ratio

An eX Twitter Eulogy

AKA fuck you, Elon.

Stephen Prime

Warning: This book is written in internet slang and bad language full of salty oaths and bitter sentiments.

Well, it is about Twitter afterall.

First published in 2024 by Hungry Wolf Press

www.hungrywolf.net

ISBN: eBook| 978-1-917595-14-8

ISBN: Paperback| 978-1-917595-15-5

A full CIP record for this book is available from the British Library.
AfullCIPrecordforthisbookisavailablefromtheLibraryofCongress.

HUNGRY WOLF PRESS
Typesetting | ProtoType
Typeset template | Will Brady
Copy Editing | Proofbot
Cover Design | Ellie Gaunt
Fact checking | Ah we'll do it later

ratio

Contents

@ThePrime8 Jun 6, 2024

We humans have an innate ability to recognise dangerous and mentally unhinged individuals and vote them into positions of power.

1 Like 1 Retweet

I quit Twitter. Not that it matters, but I had decided to quit way before the 2024 US election and subsequent exodus. I was telling my sisters about it back in August. I said I would make a book out of all my old SNS stuff. My two sisters are also very close friends, and they, unlike nearly all my other close friends, use SNS a fair bit. But not Twitter. None of my close friends were ever on Twitter. You see most of my friends live out in the countryside and they don't give a fuck about much except their strawberries in the greenhouse. But anyway, my sisters thought it was absurd to do a book of my inane posts and shitposts. Who would want to read that? That's my blood relatives. Later that night, I actually cried, I shit you not.

So why am I doing this book, and how the fuck did I manage to get it published? Good questions. Maybe you've stumbled across a tweet or two of mine over the past decade and a half. Maybe you thought this book would be funny. And if you read this far and haven't laughed yet, relax, give it time, you impatient sod. You must have heard of snippet literacy? People blamed Twitter for that, in fact they blamed it for everything. I assume that you never even liked Twitter that much either. You probably have more brain cells than you do retweets. You, I assume, like me, are an intelligent sentient human being with ideas and dreams of your own. And you probably love reading books about people like me, whose ideas and dreams are now lying obliterated on the floor in a pool of digital tears and other bodily pixel fluids, as I delete my Twitter account and try not to choke on my own resentment about the fact that nobody, nobody at all not even closest friends, gave a flying fuck about any of it.

I'm always happy to follow any online trend blindly, as part of the rearguard of course. As I said, I already had the idea of quitting first, but I am one of the last idiots to actually do it. I've just quit Twitter, made all my stuff private. Downloaded the archive. No, I don't think I'll go on Bluesky or Threads either. I am just utterly and completely over the whole fucking "microblogging" thing. Yeah, that's what people used to call it.

I joined Twitter way back in the day, on a sleepless night in London, Sep 22, 2009, 2:25 AM. As I said in one tweet marking my 15-year anniversary, "It has been literally the worst 15 years of my life". Totally not true, obviously. Call it hyperbole, or just a cry for engagement. But would more people have cared if I had been clever and said "It has been literally the most recent 15 years of my life" or something. No. Nobody ever gave a shit about me on Twitter. In those 15 years I amassed a huge following of 73 people, most of them utterly inactive, nearly catatonic accounts like my own, who never liked or retweeted me and I never followed any of them back either. Thanks, we were a great team. But I was the epitome of a sore Twitter loser. In those 15 years I wrote a total of 556 tweets, each one of them just a stupid little blurb I was hoping someone somewhere might notice and think was funny, maybe follow me.

Mind you, I did get Arnie following me once, very early on. Yes, I checked it was VERIFIED Arnie's account, like actually *Arnold Schwarzenegger*. You don't believe me, but idgaf. I even blogged about it back then, calling it a divine sign to keep writing. No, better than that, a sign from Arnie Himself.

But Arnie stopped following me when I foolishly sent Him a direct message, demanding to know why on earth He was following me, and like the better part of all our collective judgements, He's decided not to engage anymore. So, I can no longer prove it was Arnie. And the blog post I told you about. Gone. Yeah, I had trouble paying rent, let alone domain names. But seriously, why would I make that up? Oh, to make money and cash in on a lie… right. Yeah sorry, I know that's why we all quit Twitter, but take my word for it, Arnie followed me even though I wasn't following Him, and I'll tell you such a compelling tale about how and why and what happened next, you will I'm sure choose to believe me.

Because truth is now about context, now more than ever. And fuck me but Twitter was a bastard for out-of-context essentialised and minimalised shite and we all fell for it even though we must have smelled the fart jokes and the toxic masculinity for miles.

> Fact: Men get more retweets than women, even in niche circles like health services research. That's even when you take account for the fact that Twitter was always a sausage fest at 60.9% male to 39.1% female.

Here is Twitter's eulogy in <280 characters, you know for old times sakes.

> Twitter, you beautiful, broken hellscape. You gave us trends, wars, and covfefe. A digital pub where everyone yelled and nobody left sober. Now you're gone, and we're stuck explaining what a "ratio" was to future generations. Thanks for getting pixel stains all over my life. X

Btw, in case you don't know, A "ratio" on Twitter is when the number of replies to a tweet vastly outnumbers its likes and retweets. It's basically the internet's way of wrinkling its nose at a bad smell. It actually is just a simple ratio:

> Likes/Retweets > Replies = People agree or/and find it funny AF.
>
> Replies > Likes/Retweets = Noses wrinkled; people pissed.

A spectacular example you may remember was the United Airlines Incident in 2017. We all know airline companies are arseholes, and this was one of the reasons nobody (except billionaire dicks like the Virgin megaboss and NHS-suing mass killer, Richard Branson) had any sympathy when airlines were fucked by COVID.

There was a widely circulated video, equal parts tragicomedy and shocking, of a passenger who refused to get off the plane after it was overbooked. Dr. David Dao was the dude's name and he got a broken nose, though that's nothing compared to the sting from the millions of people who saw him being dragged down the aisle of the plane, as he was wrenched from his precious seat and personal dignity. In the aftermath, CEO Oscar Munoz issued a statement (a fancy word for a tweet):

> "This is an upsetting event to all of us here at United. I apologize for having to re-accommodate these customers."

That got Munoz a whopping 50,700 replies but only 6,274 likes, a stark 8:1 ratio. Haha. But who the fuck were those six thousand likes from?

The reason I'm telling you is that obviously to make this book worthy of buying, it needs to have more words than what I wrote on Twitter over the past 15 years, so I'm riffing, I'm vibing… I'm spewing facts and shitting stats to keep your attention. It's the attention economy after all and I'm bored of re-reading my tweets as well. I wanted to fit it into a broader context to make sense of it all and try to find where the last 15 years of my life went. You know after a nasty breakup, you might either a) see a therapist or b) get really drunk or c) do both over an extended period. Like that.

Here is some more interesting shit but, this time its purpose is merely to demonstrate that I actually know stuff and don't just rip off Wikipedia articles and plagiarize them for money like some fuckers out there do (yes, like you I'm sceptical of every word I read at the moment in case some lazy tosser just got ChatGPT to write it all. Though it's a lie to say I don't use an LLM when I write, as even a basic text is AI powered nowadays. Also, my grammar ability has been affected by reading stuff like "I can has cheeseburger" for way too long.

John Lennon once said, "I put things down on sheets of paper and stuff them in my pockets. When I have enough, I have a book." I found that quote in Far Out magazine, but I'm pretty sure I also read it in Barry Miles' biography of Paul McCartney. In true Lennon-esque fashion, you could say I took this ethos to heart with this little book of pixel farts. In fact, Lennon would have probably been huge on Twitter, Imagine. This short story from his first book would have been utterly spot on for Twitter:

> "A man went into a shop and bought a pair of shoes. He put them on and walked out of the shop. The shop was on fire." John Lennon, In His Own Write (1964)

I can even see exactly which .gif he'd put (KC Green's *Question Hound* in the burning house saying "This is fine").

I know this whole book sounds like a bit of a bitterness concept and a 'I could have been someone' cry drama puke fest. I know, I did Twitter all wrong. You have to be consistent, play the long game, engage people. All this shite. Who has fucking time for that? Everyone, it seems. The whole world is full of influencers now, everybody has at least 50K followers and any less makes you look pathetic. For 15 years I have had my flies down and my dick hanging out like a prat when I should have been churning out good satire, wry observation and sarcaustic wit with a ceaseless consistency like a machine or human algorithm. Instead, I was working two jobs, raising a family and moving to another country. My life was a pathetic jumble of chaos and my SNS feeds reflected the fact that most of the time I did post anything, it was when I was drunk, drunker, or drunk and bitter. In an odd way, this book is a bit of a mirror for me to hold up to myself and notice what an arsehole I've been for the last 15 years. I wanted something, but not enough to actually make it happen. I wanted followers, but I didn't know why and didn't care who. I wanted recognition, but for what? I hadn't done anything.

I'm fucking oversharing here now but that's a given. There are established links between SNS, addiction and depression. Obviously if I was drunk all the time in the last 15 years that tells you something about me. It tells *me* something about me too. Something I was clearly too drunk to notice before. I was also pretty bitter about stuff, but not proactive. This is a sign of depression, so yeah, this book is also a kind of therapy for me. If you have just quit Twitter and you are feeling blue (and I don't mean Bluesky blue, fuck that), then I hope reading these sad but hopefully very fucking funny little pixel farts and void chirps will make you realise it was all a big fucking embarrassing waste of time.

This is a curated book of my best blurt bytes and tweet splats, a Goodbye Twitter present to the world. You are very much welcome.

"A man went into a shop and bought a pair of shoes. He put them on and walked out of the shop. The shop was on fire."

John Lennon, *In His Own Write* (1964)

This is fine. Lennon would have rocked Twitter.

ERRATA

Warning: I wrote some of this book in internet slang, and I wrote some of it actually ON the internet. ~~Some~~ All of the misspellings are on purpose. Yeah, it's how we (middle-aged) young people talk. If you don't like it, you know... sorry. Who cares?

Well, actually lots of people on Twitter still do care about 'correct' language use, and misspellings and grammar fuckups were always a great source of bants. Remember "Covfefe"? 'More on that later, but the internet loves wordgoof, and they are often the origin of memes and even slang words, the obvious example being *pwned*.

Speaking of pwning, people love a bit of one-upmanship on Twitter, and inevitably there was even a @ GrammarPolice account, which was kinda funny;

> OG Tweet: "Their going to the concert without me."
>
> @ grammarpolice: "They're going to the concert without you, and you're going without proper grammar."

Interestingly, I could not find the original tweet of that, hence the tweet is missing its (not it's) date. I was also surprised that this *famous* account only has 363 followers. My gran's account has more than that! I fear this example might be an AI hallucination, but even so I like it. For some balance, here is a genuine one from them

I loved;

> @grammarpolice
>
> Sep 12, 2013
>
> Was about to correct someone's #grammar when I wondered if I only do that to overcompensate for not being good at other things.
>
> 2 Likes 1 Retweet

I looked but I couldn't find @GrammarPolice's response to the Covfefe incident. You need to know the speakers' intent to be able to correct them. Nobody to this day knows what the fuck Trump was on about when he tweeted the word, and perhaps it's better that way. No, it definitely is.

In the Japanese media, there was a recent report of a phenomena known as Time Performance (or TimePa for short), where people are watching shit speeded up 2x so they can fit more into a shorter time. People are overwhelmed at the amount of content out there, so they need a hack to get through it all.

Another thing is that it feels like I have to get this book out NOW, like YESTERDAY! It's timely now but also, I need the closure. I want to move on, do something a lot better with my life and my time. So yeah, the book went through production and all that as fast as it could. Nice but very small team at the publishers worked around the clock, but any spelling errors or factual fuckups are on me. I've indicated sources as much as I could. Spoiler alert, I don't know everything there is to know about every little thing, but I've tried to be factually close if not always bang on. Be sure to check things up. Yeah, I know you won't.

The Early Days

On the Twitternet, nobody knows if you're a poet or a pornstar, and even if they do they dgaf

THE EARLY DAYS

@ThePrime8 Dec 14, 2009

We are simultaneously the most intelligent and the most utterly stupid being on the planet.

0 Likes 0 Retweets

Rewind to 2006, a brainstorming blitz at Odeo, a podcasting company going nowhere fast. Enter Jack Dorsey, a college kid with a spark of madness and an idea: SMS as a public bullhorn, a quick ping to the universe. The result? Twitter. A platform born on 140 characters, concise and cutting, like Hemingway with a keyboard. By July that year, it roared to life.

Fast forward to 2012: 100 million users were vomiting 340 million tweets a day, raw, unfiltered thoughts, the good, the bad, and the unhinged. By 2013, Twitter was public and potent, its pulse felt across the globe. But fame is a double-edged sword. Twitter tangled with content moderation hell and a miasma of misinformation, each step forward dragging a shadow behind it.

By 2023, Twitter ceased to be Twitter. Jack's bird morphed into Musk's Frankenstein *X*. The merge, the rebrand, the cringe. It all reeks of hyper-masculine ego, a billionaire's fever dream.

Snippet Literacy: The Art of the Microburst

Twitter wasn't just a tool; it was a linguistic paradigm shift. Forget essays or manifestos, this was a sniper's platform, a place for brevity, wit, and precision. *140 characters? Make them sing*. And they did. Until they didn't.

What We Gained: Twitter taught the masses to strip their thoughts bare, sanding down verbosity to polished fragments. It was punk rock communication. Fast, raw, and searing. Anyone could shout anything they wanted into the echo chamber and enjoy the feeling flocking starlings must feel when one rando gets to be the leader of the murmuration for a few moments. I could quote Andy Warhol's 15 minutes of fame thing here but, I can't be arsed.

What We Lost: Brevity is a snake with venom in its teeth. Arguments withered into slogans, context bled dry in the name of engagement. Wit gave way to outrage; outrage became currency. Twitter made us snarky, yes, but it also made us shallow AF. The British satirists, Chris Morris & Armando Iannucci have a great phrase on their 1994 news parody *The Day Today*: "Bagpiping fact into News." You can almost hear the trumped up visual and graphic which follow that claim. It is a very apt phrase when thinking about fucking Twitter. Of course, when they named it Twitter, they knew what they were doing. Co-founder Jack Dorsey said that "twitter" means "a short burst of inconsequential information" and mimics "chirps from birds."

Two years after Twitter was inflicted upon the world, American superstar linguist Naomi Baron's 2008 book, *Always On* hit the shelves fast on its heels. She explores the concept of "Snippet Literacy," a phenomenon where digital reading and communication habits favour short, fragmented bursts of information over sustained, in-depth engagement. Baron examines how the proliferation of digital devices and online platforms shapes our approach to text and literacy, promoting skimming, scanning, and quick consumption rather than thorough understanding or deep critical thinking. Yeah, not sure what gave her that idea.

Baron beats the drum of warning, pounding out a rhythm of restless minds and fractured thoughts. She sees the long shadow of the snippet—the fast-cut, quick-fix, dopamine-hit blur of words—as a slow bleed on attention spans, an erosion of comprehension, a grindstone shaving down the brain's gears. The clash is sharp: the sleek seduction of instant knowledge versus the slow, messy labour of deep thinking, of savouring text like a meal instead of scarfing it down like junk food. What gets lost, she warns, is the marrow, the grit, the real muscle of literary and mental power. I wouldn't know anything about that, as I've been pissing my life away on Twitter for over a decade.

The C-Words: Context Collapse

I signed up for Twitter on September 22nd, 2009, 2:25 AM, London, England, Europe, Earth, Solar System, Milky Way, Universe. When you put it like that, it's clearly a very specific and yet utterly meaningless event. Who gives a fuck, right? 15 years later and the answer is still the same. No one. Not one person gave a fuck then and nobody ought to give one now, either.

But that was a relatively long time ago in the world of fast memes and trending cycles of circular reporting. And a lot has changed. Back in the day, Twitter was just as vacuous a concept then as it is now. A stupid shitty idea, originally only 140 characters! How I remember deleting and re-wording things, cutting out nuance. It was a *failnice*, a surgical idea I suppose. Perhaps Dorsey's ethos was all about cutting out the crap. Ironic, that. It was never meant to be a place where people got most of their news.

I signed up and chose a username (sprime8, original huh?), which I later changed in 2019 to @ThePrime8, but my display name was always set as **Stephen Prime**. Why did I make a Twitter account, I wonder? None of my friends, even my social-media-obsessed sisters, were on Twitter. I was heading into a new world where nobody knew me and everything I said or said I did or said I thought would be public to the world and condensed into something very easy to share. Why venture into such a weird network? For the lulz? No, sadly nothing as noble as that. I was trying to work on my career as a writer of weird edgy poems. I thought if ever there would be a market for humorous acerbic little sound bites, it would be Twitter. Back in those days, Twitter was just starting to get established.

You can read about all this on History.com by the way, which is funny as Twitter definitely is history now. It was officially launched to the public on July 15, 2006, during President George W. Bush's administration, but Bush wasn't on Twitter! No, that would have made even that warmongering sack of shit look absurd. In those early days, Twitter was already well-known as an echo chamber for idiots, and I felt right at home.

Barack Obama was the first U.S. president to use Twitter publicly, during the first-ever "Twitter Townhall @ the White House" on July 6, 2011. It had gone from inane concept for nobodies to quite an outlet. In fact, Major news corporations began adopting Twitter around the time of its public launch in 2006. The platform's real-time communication capabilities quickly attracted media outlets, which started using it to disseminate news and engage with audiences. Twitter's popularity surged, further encouraging news organizations to establish a presence on the platform.

In those days, Twitter was smol, I mean small. Yeah it was teeeeny. In 2008 it had 1.3 million registered users, which jumped to 6.9 in 2009, but the biggest growth the inane torrent of shite ever saw was in 20-fucking-10, the year after I joined. Users went up by about 800% and there were 54 million people on there. I was living in London at the time, and it felt crowded, but in the entire country there were only 63 million people.

By 2011, there were more people on Twitter than there were in the entire United Kingdom! And, amazingly despite the mass exodus we've just seen as Musk stinks the whole world up with his billionaire jism brain and onanism approach to doing business, there are still over 400 million people babbling their inane void chirps into the internet. As of recent estimates, approximately 500 million tweets are sent daily, which is about 6,000 tweets per second, 350,000 per minute, and around 200 billion tweets a fucking year. And of course, we all know it blows up regularly, with big spikes during major events like the world cup or... I don't know, let me see... a major presidential election.

My first ever tweet looked like this:

> @ThePrime8 Sep 22, 2009
>
> I am updating my website www.stephenprime.com - check out visuals for tortoise roadkill on youtube
>
> 0 Likes 0 Retweets

I must have been very happy to get a few followers on Twitter, but really my writing at the time was very vitriolic (yeah, worse than now even) and I was quite fond of the old C word. This is just a warning that if you search the net you can probably find a fair few C bombs. But, in the late 2010s in Britain I must say the C word was shocking but it was hardly something you could get cancelled for. However, I felt it was a mark of the type of people I could engage with; namely people who used expletive language and mother fucking big grown up swear words. Studies have shown that creative swearing is actually a sign of intelligence, btw. There is a book by Emma Byrne called

Swearing Is Good For You: The Amazing Science of Bad Language and it says so in there. Fucking good book.

That's a bit of context for what happened next:

@ThePrime8 Sep 22, 2009

life is lethal in large doses - new short story

0 Likes 0 Retweets

@ThePrime8 Sep 22, 2009

Searched "cunt" and followed everyone who used it in the last 10 mins. Result: cunts everywhere!

0 Likes 0 Retweets

In my infinite wisdom I had searched the C word and found a bunch of people who had used it, then I followed them all. Sadly, this brought me into contact with lots of fellow idiots, regardless of their ideas or interests.

What these delightfully playful and random experiments with social media achieved were to poison my Twitter algorithm, which at the time I didn't know anything about and to this day is still a closely held corporate secret as to how it actually fucking works.

The other thing I did was to search for a bunch of porn stars and follow NOT the stars but the people who were openly following these porn stars on Twitter. One such dude was called cacacowboy69 (handle changed for anonymity, why I have no idea the guy's public on Twitter).

@ThePrime8 Sep 25, 2009

found this amazing horny nutter called cacacowboy69. This guy is ace, check out his page!

0 Likes 0 Retweets

@ThePrime8 Sep 26, 2009

My guy cacacowboy69 is perving like a mother fucker. Know any other good weirdos to follow?

0 Likes 0 Retweets

Sure, don't get me started on porn, but I personally wouldn't want my public Twitter account to be associated with porn stars, as people would then have hard proof of the fact that I'm a total wanker. It interested me from an anthropological perspective, that these wankers were openly following their idols. Openly being wankers. That takes balls, or similar equipment. Or stupidity. I suppose it could be a lot more embarrassing, say if you were following Justin Bieber or somebody. That would be very shameful shit, right there.

I thought this was fun and subversive at the time, and maybe it was? Maybe not. But it did create a very difficult and unpredictable pattern of behaviour for my account right off the bat. The Twitter engine had no idea how to place me, as even now I've explained it, the lack of logic is rather evident. Nice job, younger me. I guess I deserved those 15 years in the microblogging wilderness for that.

However, I will say this: there were some sweet and tender moments I observed a few times in those early days, as the porn-follower people would say night night to the starlet stars they loved, and a lot of the stars would tweet photos of themselves with no makeup or just cuddling up with a cat and a book on a rainy day. You know, humanising stuff. And the audience didn't tweet smutty requests to these people (well, probably a lot of them did). No they were sending night night hugs and kisses back. It made me realise that no matter how sad and pathetic you are, people still just want to be loved. I would also like to say that I did start following one ex-adult star, Aurora Snow, as she became a very real journalist who covers the sex industry with an insiders' perspective.

It was clear even then that on the Twitternet, nobody knows if you're a poet or a pornstar, and even if they do, they dgaf. You can still be anything you want and get likes. Unless you're me, that is. I got nothing. Now the problem with all these shenanigans is that they play right at the razor-sharp edge of the buzzsaw Venn diagram of context collapse.

DAFUQ IS CONTEXT COLLAPSE?

@ThePrime8 Oct 16, 2009

Imaginative ways to get fired: 1 come to work dressed as a toilet brush and head barge your boss' arse

0 Likes 0 Retweets

This tweet gives you some idea why I use a pen name. I

don't want my boss knowing I once contemplated sticking my head up their arse. Anonymity on SNS is sometimes as vital as a VPN. It's all about context.

Context collapse is a phenomenon that occurs when social media flattens the boundaries between different audiences, forcing individuals to address multiple groups simultaneously. A kind of digital blender, if you will. Coined by danah boyd (yes her name is spelled with a lower-case b), a social media scholar, and elaborated by Alice Marwick, it describes the merging of diverse social contexts—family, friends, coworkers, and strangers—into a single, undifferentiated audience.

Imagine telling a joke to your close friends. Now, imagine telling that same joke to your grandmother, your boss, and a room full of strangers. What might land as humour with one group could bomb spectacularly with another. On platforms like Twitter, where posts are often public and easily shared, this "flattening" of audiences means users must navigate the impossible task of addressing everyone at once. Imagine, say, a teacher on Twitter a few drinks in, he sees one of his students and they start a discussion. See the problem? Normally pissed up teachers don't frat with brats, but this time? Things could even get flirty, or downright dirty.

boyd and Marwick argue that context collapse creates unique challenges in managing self-presentation. In face-to-face communication, we adjust our language, tone, and even topics based on who we're talking to. Social media strips away these nuances, replacing tailored communication with broadcast-style messages. This can lead to misunderstandings, unintentional offense, or the oversimplification of complex ideas for fear of backlash.

For example, a tweet intended as an in-joke for friends might be interpreted differently or go viral among strangers. This could be an invitation for criticism and harassment. Celebrities and influencers are especially vulnerable to context collapse, as their audiences are a patchwork of fans, detractors, and casual observers.

Context collapse also complicates authenticity. Marwick and boyd note that balancing multiple identities for disparate audiences can feel performative, leading some users to curate an online persona that sacrifices sincerity for safety or broad appeal. This balancing act highlights the tension between being “authentic” and managing one’s image in the face of countless, unseen viewers.

Ultimately, context collapse isn’t just a technical issue, it’s a cultural one. It reshapes how we think about audiences, identity, and communication in the digital age. Platforms thrive on collapsing contexts, as viral content benefits from reaching as many people as possible, but the human cost, stress, miscommunication, and performative identity, remains an unresolved consequence of our hyperconnected world.

And now, what we see is contexts being folded into datasets of staggering size full of information about users’ habits, shopping and movement, spending, beliefs, political ideologies and whatever the fuck else there is a table for on the database. It’s scary but some governments have already weaponised this information on their populace in order to control and subjugate the masses. Fuck me, that sounds like a conspiracy theory but it's actually just how things are in China with their Social Credit System. What would George Orwell make of all this? And would Orwell have been able to come up with anything as absurd and inane as this tweet:

> @ThePrime8 Dec 14, 2009
>
> We are simultaneously the most intelligent and the most utterly stupid being on the planet.
>
> 0 Likes 0 Retweets

Finding my voice

OK, now we get to the real black centipede meat. These are just a few of the inane things I chose to tweet from those early days. I categorised them, but basically, they're just floating here in the middle of the end of the beginning of this book like the idiotic dangleberries they are.

DEEP

Thought this category would impress you all.

Profound AF.

> @ThePrime8 Nov 11, 2009
>
> if you see an x-ray of yourself, is that the real you? are we just living bones witj nothing but black inside. a vacuum inside white bone
>
> 0 Likes 0 Retweets

I only had one profound one.

DARK

Loads more in this category. Obviously, sometimes I was quite low and made my sad and bleak views public, wanting perhaps to bring down other people with me in a pathetic and sad, lonely public display of emotion. Luckily, absolutely nobody noticed.

> @ThePrime8 Mar 30, 2010
>
> life is a hollow hole we fuck ourselves into and prematurely ejaculate.
>
> 0 Likes 0 Retweets

Wonder why nobody liked that one?

> @ThePrime8 Mar 24, 2010
>
> Broken inhibitions, sex clones with 6 cocks and 7 cunts fucking in 0-Gravity while the camera does an oscilloscope on the action from behind
>
> 0 Likes 0 Retweets

I think someone actually made that film. Full disclosure though I was probably trying to promote my poem called Porn Clones, which isn't in this book but it was published as a video on YouTube and unlike my other poems, has yet to be taken down, because is has way more views than any of my other videos simply on account of how porn obsessed people are on YouTube. Horrid little vidiwankers.

> @ThePrime8 Nov 10, 2009
>
> What would you rather eat - dog shit or human shit? What does that say about humans?
>
> 0 Likes 0 Retweets

Well, you can infer from the above that I would rather eat dog shit than human shit. I did ask someone else this, and they replied with a bit too much thought, saying it depends on what the human or the dog had eaten in the past 12-24 hours.

> @ThePrime8 Nov 4, 2009
>
> As cristmas approaches, so do the roaches *www.stephenprime.com*
>
> 0 Likes 0 Retweets

I am actually hoping to get this book ready before xmas this year, so you can stick it in the bottom of your stockings and never look at it again (non Christmassy Edit: I am currently fucked on New Year's Eve Eve and hoping to some-fucking-how launch this egg of twitter sperm shit out of my brain and into your mind-womb… fuck all of this will make sense if you ever read to the end, but christ I do NOT want any fucking TWITTER in my 2025, no thanks, no!).(!) [[php? Shortcode, grammar, logic?]]

Arnie

As a kid growing up in the 80s, Arnie was He-Man for me. Well, now I'm a grown-up, he's no longer He-Man but he is THE man. And one day back in 2009 I logged into Twitter and saw my measly follower count had gone up yet again. In my excitement, I posted the following.

@ThePrime8 Oct 15, 2009

I must be awesome - Arnold Schwarzenegger is following me

0 Likes 0 Retweets

OK, I know you won't believe me, and I can no longer prove this, but it really was really the REAL real Arnie. How do I know? I clicked the profile and it had a little blue seal next to it. That's how I knew. I checked this, and the "Verified Accounts" program on Twitter was set up in June 2009, so the dates link up. It was created, incidentally, after the void chirp dispensary was dissed by Kanye West and sued by Tony La Russa over unauthorized fake-ass accounts run by impersonators.

So, what did I do next? I wrote a blog post about it, as if it was a sign from god. Actually I respect Arnie even more than god. Not his politics or his extra-marital affairs, his muscles and his movies, his cool sense of humour and the fact that he did it all with English as his second language. So what did I do? I sent him a Direct Message:

@ThePrime8 Oct 15, 2009, 2.53 AM

Hey! You've made my day! What made you click follow? Was it Ant Monkeys?

I sent him a link to my *Ant Monkeys* poetry video. Don't bother searching for that though, YouTube took it down on Sun, 19 Dec 2021, claiming my poem about how the human race was a horrible destructive species that live out of balance with the Earth was "hate speech". I appealed but they said it still was. FYI, my *Ant Monkeys* poem has the C word in, but then so does Alan Ginsberg's *Sunflower Sutra*. I know this is one of those excuses, but *Ant Monkeys* was originally published in a zine called The Vein, which was edited by a very wonderful young woman named Jami Kali and she had no problem with the language. I just searched for it though, and surprise surprise, it is long gone and Jami has changed her last name, presumably she's grown up a lot more than I have since then. Talk about the ephemeral nature of shit online.

As you can guess, Arnie never replied and he is no-longer following me. But it doesn't matter. I was on Arnie's radar, for a while, once upon a time. I also once left a printout of my poems with the doorman of Bruce Willis' New York apartment. If Bruce ever did get those poems, maybe that's what caused his tragic memory illness.

Back to 2009, Arnie following me was all I could tweet about:

> @ThePrime8 Oct 16, 2009
>
> Awesome. Arnie is still following me. I rock
>
> 0 Likes 0 Retweets

@ThePrime8 Oct 22, 2009

Wow - First Arnie following me on Twitter, now Jim Carey is my freind on facebook. I'm ace. *www.stephenprime.com*

0 Likes 0 Retweets

@ThePrime8 Oct 22, 2009

Actually, now I'm not sure it is the real Jim Carey. At least I know Arnie is for real.

0 Likes 0 Retweets

@ThePrime8 Oct 29, 2009

this guy called apocalypse is following me - he's almost as ace as Schwarzenegger (who is also following me, btw)

0 Likes 0 Retweets

@ThePrime8 Nov 5, 2009

Hey Twitter-bugs, what is the point. The only people who read my blogs are porn hoes and ca$h bloggers (oh, and Arnie) *www.stephenprime.com*

0 Likes 0 Retweets

@ThePrime8 Mar 23, 2010

Blogging and tweeting is so utterly pointless, if it weren't for the fact arnie is following me i'd have nothing to say to you arseholes.

0 Likes 0 Retweets

Now, this might look inane to you, but my friends at the time thought the story was funny. However, they also did NOT believe me about Arnie and they were so disgusted by my Twitter project that they couldn't even be bothered to create an account to check, and, you know maybe follow me? No, they were all much too high and mighty for Twitter and they stayed clean and pure. My escapades on Twitter had started to warp me.

Lashing out at my followers, not cool, right? Wrong. One guy on Twitter, the Mozart to my Salieri, was doing just that and getting phat likes. His name was Wint back then, and his handle was @dril.

@dril Jul 12, 2020

my followers are STUPID as FUCK !!! they are all on CRANK !!! they hate ALL my shit!!!

18K Likes 1.5K Retweets & 144 fucking comments!! wtf

Who was this guy and why wasn't he... me?

THE MIDDLE BIT

slow internet is a sign that you have masturbated enough and it's time for other people to have their turn

THE MIDDLE BIT

@ThePrime8 Aug 29, 2019

Technically, you can't not give a fuck unless it's from the fuque region of France, otherwise it's just sparkling indifference.

0 Likes 0 Retweets

From 2011 to 2019, Twitter was like a chaotic dinner party where revolutions, memes, and petty arguments all fought for the last slice of attention pie. 2011 brought the Arab Spring, where Twitter flexed its muscles as a tool for real political change, briefly tricking everyone into thinking the platform would save humanity. By 2014, we were retweeting Ellen's Oscar selfie while brands discovered "personality" and started tweeting like unhinged teenagers.

Then Trump arrived in 2016, turned Twitter into his personal megaphone, and made 280 characters feel like 280 grenades thrown into the media cycle daily. Meanwhile, misinformation skyrocketed, bots infiltrated every hashtag, and Dril noisily held the fort of Weird Twitter with his absurdist bullshit. By 2019, Twitter had fully evolved into its final form: half town square, half gladiator pit. Moments of genuine connection or wit were drowned in outrage, algorithms, and 24-hour memes. It wasn't all bad, just mostly exhausting.

By 2011 I had moved from London to Tokyo. As the famous literary critic, essayist and dictionary dude, Samuel Johnson once said, "When a man is tired of London, he is tired of life, for there is in London all that life can afford." Well, I couldn't afford to fucking live in London anymore.

> @ThePrime8 Nov 26, 2009
>
> the taste of london like a used condom sandwich. gutless lawyers and bankers thrive along with the rats and the politicians
>
> 0 Likes 0 Retweets

In moving to Japan, my pool of English-speaking friends got smaller, and it was far away, AND totally out of time-sync. Timing is important on SNS for engagement, there are websites that you can use to calculate the perfect fucking time to unleash a post. Yeah, I know about them, they didn't help me at all. In moving to Tokyo, I had moved into the future, and as we look back we know that the future is fucking fucked and not a good place right now.

In this section I'll tell you all about how Twitter became too big for its own huge torrent of shite, and how I wrestled with jealousy and indifference.

@dril

In the last chapter, I said Dril was Mozart to my Salieri. I mean that's funny and shit but, come on. Mozart? Everyone knows Mozart was overrated. If you've been paying attention (which no doubt you haven't because of Snippet Literacy and the Attention Economy) you will remember that I started MY account on 22nd September 2009.

Dril started his account on September 15th 2008. At the time of writing, Dril has 14.2K posts and a whopping 1.7 Million followers. And while the mystique once suggested nobody knew who he was, the poor dude got fucking doxxed (something to do with rights when he wanted to publish a book of his tweets, great idea!) and it was revealed that Dril is Paul Dochney, a 30-something man from New Jersey who, in an interview with *The Ringer*, mentioned he earns about "as much money as a Kmart manager or something."

Dril is known for his absurdist humour, and has been a significant figure in online culture since his account's inception.

Notable tweets:

- "No."
  Dril's inaugural tweet, simply stating "No," which I somehow will link to a story about John Lennon meeting Yoko Ono at some other point in this book.
- "Who the hell is scraeming 'LOG OFF' at my house. show yourself, coward. i will never log off."

That wasn't me, I promise.

- "if your grave doesnt say 'rest in peace' on it you are automatically drafted into the skeleton war." I think there was an actual game made from this tweet. I dunno but I definitely want to be part of the skeleton army so when I die make sure my grave clearly indicates my rank and status, I want to be a fat rich skeleton commander.

During the COVID-19 pandemic, Dril used Patreon to fund a game he was making, which seems to be called *Viral Dominion* and I think is perhaps still in development. He also produced a HUGE book titled *The Get Rich and Become God Method*. If you sub to his Patreon, you can listen to his *Final Mouth* podcast. I believe that he's also got some projects with Adult Swim to make a TV show. To be honest I don't really care anymore. I'm over it.

Alls you need to know is this; Dril is basically the de facto god of Weird Twitter. When Musk made Twitter X and started asking people to pay to get a blue seal next to their name, Dril got one for free and he had them remove it, made a big war out of it. He's very anti-Musk and we seem to see eye to eye politically, but unlike me he could actually fill a book with all his Tweets, my conservative estimate is that at 100 words per tweet he'd be looking at nearly quarter of a million words with his 14K tweets. My 556 tweets added up to a mere 8,286 words. It's like looking in a fucking mirror, a mirror to another dimension. Or, actually it's like someone sent me out to buy booze and when I got back to the party, it's descended into a brilliant orgy, but the doors are locked and all I can do is watch through the window. With the booze, of course. At least I did have that.

The inaugural "NO" tweet reminds me of another John Lennon thing, and in fact wow, I just remembered how I found out about Dril in the first place. Strap in for the narrative.

Dril has just under 2 million followers, not too shabby eh? But not massive either. The GrEaT man himself had this to say on the matter:

> @dril Jun 27, 2023
>
> realized having 2000000 ***followers*** is a bad idea when i posted about being sawed in half by a car & a guy got mad at me bc it happened to him
>
> 13K Likes 660K Retweets & 47 comments

A funny riff, he is actually talking about context collapse there. Speaking of saying whatever the fuck you want without fearing the consequences, for perspective, the @realDonaldTrump handle had 88.7 million followers when his account was officially suspended in January 2021. I just checked again (November 2024) and the man has 95 million followers. That's a lot of fucking people. As far as I can tell, there are only like 13 countries in the world with populations higher than that. So he has more followers than most countries have people.

With only a small (2 million, I'd have been happy with 2 thousand!) followers, Dril was a bit niche perhaps. This is how I heard of Dril. I lied before when I said none of my close friends use Twitter. I mean, I'm from Yorkshire but we do have electricity up in the hills. I had exactly one friend who used Twitter, and he was actually pretty big too, even had a viral tweet once, 50k likes. Anyway, I think I was telling him about how John Lennon met Yoko Ono.

It was 1966, an art exhibition in London where gravity bent. Yoko Ono was the artist, and Lennon was impressed with the stepladder that had a magnifying glass at the top and a tiny little note simply reading "Yes." Lennon peers through a magnifying glass, pleased that it didn't say "No." When he asked Yoko Ono, "What's this about?" she just smirked and fired back, "That's for you." The kind of minimalist cheek that sends one marriage to the grave and births a counterculture storm.

Historians can't lock down the story's source. It's a mystery swirled in anecdotes and Lennon's scattered interviews. I think maybe I read it in Barry Miles's book *Many Years From Now*, but who knows? The lore is stickier than the truth.

I told my Twitter friend about this and he told me the thing about Dril's first ever "NO" tweet. You see, if only I'd thought of that. Ever since, a professional rivalry was born, one that Dril never even noticed. He was so high up there on his 2 million followers that he couldn't even see me all the way down there trying.

I even @ed him a couple of times;

> @ThePrime8 Jul 27, 2019
>
> its your fault that its my fault @dril
>
> 0 Likes 0 Retweets

I guess I was trying to troll people, surprised the GrammarPolice didn't pick me up for that one.

@ThePrime8 Mar 4, 2021

how can i get as many followeas as @dril without bothering to tweet all that inane shite

0 Likes 0 Retweets

Mind you, it's gotta be tough up top as well:

@dril Jun 15, 2023

Frankly many of my followers are Dirty and Stupid , and only pretend to understand the significance of my Posts.

5.8K Likes 675K Retweets & 97 comments

But he must feel like a right prick now, millions of followers on Twitter is like Enron shares (there has to be an Elon pun in there somewhere). I see that of late, Dril is fulltime trying to troll X over that stupid blue seal that you have to pay for. He gets it free as the king of Weird Twitter, but he asked them to remove it. Pretty boss retro cocaine Miami vice vibes when you look at the high-resolution retro promotional materials, with the rolled up sleeves and bright suits. Nice but, yeah you're not going home with MY daughter, punk. Hey Dril, I bought your book of tweets, and I would buy another! LMK if you need a ghost writer, DM me dude.

Also, remember that introductory tweet of Dril's from all those pages ago? Remember ratios as well? I ran the maths:

- Likes to Retweets Ratio:
    - 18,000 Likes / 1,500 Retweets = 12:1
    - For every retweet, there are 12 likes. Solid like-to-retweet ratio; people enjoyed it but didn't feel it was worth amplifying.
- Comments to Likes Ratio:
    - 144 Comments / 18,000 Likes = 0.008:1 (or ~1 comment per 125 likes)
    - The comment section is chill for the like count, rarely the case on the internet. Either uncontroversial or a vibe everyone agrees with.
- Comments to Retweets Ratio:
    - 144 Comments / 1,500 Retweets = 0.096:1 (~1 comment per 10 retweets)
    - Decent harmony here; people aren't diving in to start a beef.

Overall? This post is resonating more for passive consumption (likes) than conversation (comments) or sharing (retweets). It's either wholesome, funny, or so agreeable it escaped the fiery maw of Twitter discourse. I will admit that despite nearly 2 million followers, I have to believe that Dril does in fact have an accurate summation of his earnings. Glamourous influencer? It seems that even if you're famous, if you're weird it's hard to be rich.

So, although he won, I didn't lose. Now I'm going to do something really fun and repurpose something Salieri said in a conversation with Hüttenbrenner on June 8, 1822, quoted in Alexander Wheelock Thayer's book, Salieri: rival of Mozart (1989):

> I feel that the end of my days is drawing near; my senses are failing me; my delight and strength in creating tweets are gone; he (Dril), who was once honoured by half of Europe, is forgotten; others have come and are the objects of admiration; one must give place to another.

Srsly Dril, DM me. I love you.

I don't really know where to put all my tweets

Turns out one of the reasons I didn't get any likes on Twitter was that some of my best stuff wasn't even on there; it was for friends only on Facebook. And I didn't even have a Patreon tier. I'm my own worst enemy sometimes.

> July 18, 2017 Facebook
>
> Feel like I've been shat through the bowels of an asp

> June 14 2018 Facebook
>
> Don't make the mistake of getting drunk and then assuming that everyone else is as drunk as you. Because they're not. They're really not.

January 2, 2018 Facebook

fuck. now my slippers are gonna smell like gin

June 14, 2017 Facebook

I'm all hatey today

@ThePrime8 Jan 25, 2019

#need #advice #about #how #to #use #hastags

0 Likes 0 Retweets

@ThePrime8 Sep 24, 2017

My internal monologue has Tourette's

0 Likes 0 Retweets

@ThePrime8 Jun 15, 2018

Idea for a film. Here and Learning in Las Vegas: A guy travels with his teacher (played by Kevin Spacey) to Las Vegas where they spend a lot of time watching people play dice to learn about maths and statistics. Then they drive home.

0 Likes 0 Retweets

@ThePrime8 December 14, 2017

Fuck the ubiquity of stupidity

0 Likes 0 Retweets

@ThePrime8 December 14, 2017

I hate a lotta stuff. One of them is everything

0 Likes 0 Retweets

December 14, 2017 Facebook

No one cares about me so neither do I

My dad liked that one for me, which is nice. Cheers pops.

June 30th, 2017 Facebook

Smarmy friend: OK, if you're so arty and clever, name an artist from Denmark

Me [effortlessly off top of my head]: Asger Jorn

Smarmy friend: who is your smarmy friend

Me: It's me. This is my own internal monologue

Smarmy friend: [I win face]

When I had 69 followers

At one point I had 69 and that was my favourite number, for… whatever puerile reason. At that point I actually requested no more followers please.

> @ThePrime8 Jan 22, 2019
>
> PLEASE, nobody else follow me as I have exactly 69 followers and I like it that way
>
> 0 Likes 0 Retweets

I was hoping people would call my bluff and I would go viral. Only four more people joined up in the year or two that followed, hence the 73, but funnily I must have got 2 followers just for the 69 thing, which I now realise isn't bad considering my paltry stats in the first place. Still, I wasn't happy about it.

> @ThePrime8 Jan 25, 2019
>
> now it's gone up to 71 followers. You bastards ruined all the fun
>
> 0 Likes 0 Retweets

This could be on a fucking T-Shirt

Twitter's inanity has always been ripe for satire, and plenty of people made careers or cult followings by skewering the platform's absurdities. Some did it with surrealist humour, à la Dril. Others turned to music, like Sleaford Mods with their 2014 track "Tweet Tweet Tweet."

Ironically it's one of their most famous tracks, but imho it's shit compared to some of their other belters, like Blog Maggot or Jobseeker. Still, the line "All you zombies, tweet tweet tweet" resonates sufficiently to get an angry middle-aged nod from most people.

Now, if I didn't think there were some merits to Twitter, I would never have gone on there, would I? I'm not an idiot. Well, I am an idiot, obviously, but an idiot really just means an ordinary person. Seriously, in ancient Greece and Rome the word "idiot" (idiōtēs) originally meant "a private person" or "a common man". It did not have an insulting connotation at the time.

And although I'm saying all this shit about how I sucked at Twitter, really though in my heart of fucking hearts, I know some of this is funny. It's funny to me, at least. Here for a bit more filler are some of the funniest tweets I wrote to an astonishing wall of indifference.

Unless otherwise stated, all of these amazingly poignant tweets I wrote got a big fat ZERO in the likes department.

> @ThePrime8 Nov 11, 2013
>
> Be unique, just like everybody else.
>
> 0 Likes 0 Retweets

I actually think that one is pretty good. I'm quite sure it's been said before, but I said it that way in 2013 and nobody batted even one of their beautiful unique eyelashes. Sods.

@ThePrime8 Oct 3, 2013

It's a shame I'm not ashamed of myself

0 Likes 0 Retweets

I don't know what I had done to be ashamed, or not ashamed… but I am quite proud of the oxymoron.

@ThePrime8 Jun 10, 2013

The only things that matter to me are the things that matter #pointless

0 Likes 0 Retweets

Another trite little saying. I think that's about as deep as you can really go with 140 characters (Twitter moved to 280 characters in November 2017).

@ThePrime8 Feb 4, 2013

So funny I shit my pants. No shit.

0 Likes 0 Retweets

If you don't know whether to believe I actually shit myself and then posted it on one of the largest, open and viewable-by-anyone-in-the-world social networks that has ever existed with a user-base that now encompasses 12.6% of the world's internet users, then read on as there's a lot more.

@ThePrime8 May 18, 2012

The universe is a fucked up place. I wouldn't want to live there.

0 Likes 0 Retweets

Come on, that's funny… because. Oh, never mind.

@ThePrime8 Jan 20, 2012

The universe is the most unfriendly place on earth.

0 Likes 0 Retweets

Similar cosmic theme. I think *Prometheus* had just come out. Oh no, that was later that year on August 24th. So just random cosmic capers then.

@ThePrime8 Jan 23, 2012

Excruciating relief

0 Likes 0 Retweets

A cryptic tweet, don't even remember what it was about but perhaps I was referring to when my big toenail fell off. It's mystifying but it's nowhere near Covfefe.

@ThePrime8 Dec 4, 2009

News flash: no one gives a shit

0 Likes 0 Retweets

I mean, come on, that's a good one? Not even a single like? If Dril had posted that he'd have 3M followers by now.

@ThePrime8 Aug 29, 2019

Technically, you can't not give a fuck unless it's from the fuque region of France, otherwise it's just sparkling indifference.

0 Likes 0 Retweets

I actually turned that one into a meme, with the correct smug template and everything. Still no likes. Also, that meme was trending at the time, the whole 'Technically,' thing. But I truly was met with sparkling indifference.

> @ThePrime8 Feb 3, 2019
>
> Guess what!! Something nobody gives a fuck about has happened!!!!!!!
>
> 1 Like 0 Retweets

> @ThePrime8 Feb 3, 2019
>
> Don't piss on my strawberries
>
> 0 Likes 0 Retweets

I just found the juxtaposition of strawberries and piss very funny.

> @ThePrime8 Feb 3, 2019
>
> BastardFuck-a-SaurusRex
>
> 0 Likes 0 Retweets

Remember how creative swearing is a sign of intelligence, according to that book from before I mentioned. Yeah, it clearly doesn't apply to me.

I hope you bastards don't steal any of these slogans and put them on a T-Shirt. My publisher joked that they are selling merch now if you want. Personally, I don't need your landfill on my conscience, but feel free to spend a penny on my behalf.

Note for anyone not as old and less British than me, *spend a penny means* to go for a piss. That's because in Britain we charge you to use the public lavs. Even our piss has been lining the pockets of the ruling elite for at least a few centuries. Oh, speaking of corruption, capitalism and rich rulers…

Covfefe

@ThePrime8 Feb 3, 2019

Fuck all cheezy orange fuck-witted things

0 Likes 0 Retweets

2017. Six minutes after midnight, Eastern Time, on May 31st, Trump tweeted "Despite the constant negative press covfefe".

Six hours later, the tweet was gone, but the fallout? Still radioactive. It was a masterclass in presidential eloquence. A profound statement, no doubt, leaving the world in awe of its... clarity.

Covfefe lingered for a solid 360 minutes before vanishing into the digital abyss, but not before igniting a wildfire of internet mockery. White House Press Secretary Sean Spicer, in a valiant attempt to maintain the mystique, claimed, "The president and a small group of people know exactly what he meant." Of course, because who wouldn't understand such a lucid proclamation?

There were sooooooo many hilarious memes and riffs and jokes. So many that it wouldn't be my place to curate them all. I've got 500 of my tweets in this book to worry about, and surprisingly not one of them mentioned Covfefe. It's like this one little word paralysed my satire engine and sent me into meltdown. In 2017 I was also finishing my PhD irl so maybe that had something to do with it. But even though I am an actual Doctor of Philosophy (in linguistics no less!) I still have no idea what this word fucking means.

In the grand tapestry of internet blunders, "covfefe" remains a shining beacon, reminding us all of the perils of late-night tweeting without a proofreader. But, to be honest, one thing nobody else commented on was the fact that Trump's grammar and spelling in all his other torrents of insane and toxic tweets is actually pretty much spot on. Very few of them would have riled the @GrammarPolice. Maybe having good grammar is overrated? The fruits of an expensive education, perhaps? He knows nothing about reality, but he knows how to use an apostrophe.

COVID

Oh fuck, here we go. Hold tight. We all remember this was the turning point in many of our lives, as shit got real bad real quick and never really got better.

> @ThePrime8 Mar 24, 2020
>
> slow internet is a sign that you have masturbated enough and it's time for other people to have their turn #boredathome #sarcasm #humour
>
> 0 Likes 0 Retweets

OK I was going to write a whole thing about this. Remember in 2016 how the saddest shit we could focus on was a spate of dead celebrities? Then in 2019 we were feeling super bleak and we couldn't really imagine how shit could get any worse? Remember?

The world didn't just go to hell in 2020, it went all Piper Perri. Trump was bleating "FRAUD!" like a cartoon goat from those trippy 1950s cartoons. He refused to leave the Oval Office, a toddler with nuclear codes clutching his toys. George Floyd's murder once again laid bare the need to specifically state that #BlackLivesMatter, and the streets erupted in protests that bled across the globe, fists raised against police brutality and systemic rot.

Meanwhile, Australia burned, California burned, and the air choked on the ash of climate collapse. While billionaires like Bezos raked in record profits, the rest of us were scraping burnt crusts of sourdough from the pan, praying our Wi-Fi didn't drop. Essential workers were called "heroes," but we treated them like cannon fodder, working until their lungs gave out for a paycheck that couldn't even cover rent.

Isolation ate us alive, too. Anxiety and depression skyrocketed while Zoom calls replaced hugs. Homes became prisons. Every wall inched closer, every screen glared brighter, every doomscroll another nail in the coffin of sanity. It was too much to take, too much to process. The centre didn't just fail to hold, it imploded, and the shrapnel is still lodged in all of us.

A PANDEMIC OF TWEETS

The pandemic hit like a hammer, blunt and unrelenting. One moment, I was living in a world where Twitter was a constant hum of memes, arguments, and overlong threads. The next, it was ground zero for every ounce of fear, confusion, and righteous fury humanity could muster. By March 2020, my feed was a deluge of uncertainty: bread recipes alongside grim hospital stats, and "flatten the curve" hashtags next to rants about toilet paper hoarding. It was chaos, and I was both too online and not online enough to deal with it.

I wasn't tweeting as much. Odd, considering I had more time. The world stopped, yet somehow, I felt heavier, slower. For some reason I didn't really feel like going on Twitter. A pandemic will do that to you.

CORONAGEDDON #coronavirus #fuck #bored

That was my mood, a putrid mix of bored, cynical, and trying to wring humour out of the madness. But let's be honest, the energy to engage wasn't there. Twitter, for all its dopamine hits, was exhausting. I tried to play along. People were dying. Whole cities shut down. What did my little quips matter?

The pandemic should have been a golden age for content. Instead, it became a reckoning. I scrolled endlessly, absorbing news, rumours, and whatever nonsense my timeline spit out. And oh, the nonsense. Conspiracies flowed faster than hand sanitizer: masks don't work, 5G towers cause COVID, Bill Gates is out here microchipping us with vaccines. I didn't know whether to laugh or cry.

And then, of course, there was Trump. "China virus," he called it. Over and over again. He poured gasoline on the fire of racism and misinformation with every tweet. My timeline devolved into shouting matches, hashtags like #KungFlu trending alongside calls for compassion. I hated him, and I hated how his words infected everything. But I was also a victim of racism myself, even as a white dude. You see I live in Japan (a fact I find so mundane I rarely remember to cash in on it). And out here I'm a minority, and specifically English speaking people were the target of COVID-based racism.

In the throes of the pandemic, Japanese TV decided to break the internet by serving up a gem of absurdity. A national television program called *Hiruobi!* aired a segment that quickly became infamous, and is still viewable on YouTube. The show featured a demonstration claiming that English speakers, with their explosive "P" sounds, were propelling viral particles further than the more subdued Japanese pronunciation. To demonstrate, a woman stood with a paper clipped before her face, intoning “Kore wa pen desu” (the Japanese for “this is a pen”). The paper fluttered gently. Then, she unleashed the English “This is a pen,” and the paper flew back as if struck by a gale. The implication? English was a linguistic super-spreader. It encapsulated everything Twitter was: a machine that turns molehills into mountains, sometimes with disastrous results.

Twitter seized upon this with glee. Parodies emerged, exaggerating the force of English plosives to comedic extremes. One viral video juxtaposed the phrase with scenes of tsunamis and typhoons, suggesting that uttering “pen” in English could unleash natural disasters. The internet’s collective sarcasm was a sight to behold, but this was one of those fine examples of how we all split into niches online, but even more so during COVID.

Yet, beneath the humour lay a critique of pseudoscience and the absurd lengths media would go to explain complex phenomena, especially if they could blame a particular group. Us and Them. The segment became a meme, a shorthand for the ridiculousness of oversimplified explanations during a global crisis.

Even in a pandemic, the world found time to mock the trivial, to laugh at the ludicrous. “This is a pen” became a symbol of the surreal times we were living through and a reminder that, amidst the chaos, even a privileged white British expat living in Tokyo could end up feeling that he was being discriminated against. Imagine how those other fuckers felt who were genuinely being targeted for serious racial abuse and profiling.

Twitter was at once too much and not enough. Every swipe was a fresh wound. Information overload replaced meaningful connection. There were moments of clarity, sure, but mostly it was noise. I thought I'd tweet more during lockdown, but what was there to say? "Oh good, it was only a one-off shart then," I posted in June, but my shart tweets never did well, like the real-life incident they were based on, they were funny but ultimately nobody liked them.

The pandemic didn't inspire me to create. It drained me. Twitter became a place to witness the chaos, not contribute to it. And yet, I kept scrolling, chasing clarity in a fog of hashtags and despair.

THE VIRUS OF FAKE NEWS

Twitter turned into a petri dish in 2020, amplifying not just the virus but the misinformation that clung to it like a parasite. It started slow. Posts from earnest doctors and government accounts laid out the basics: wash your hands, stay six feet apart, wear a mask. Simple stuff. But then the cracks appeared. Conspiracies sprouted like mould in the damp corners of the internet, each one more bizarre than the last.

I remember scrolling past a tweet claiming masks didn't work because viruses are "smaller than mask fibres." Someone quote-tweeted it with, "So is your fart, but you still wear pants." I laughed, then cried a little inside, because millions of people were taking posts like that seriously.

The Bill Gates vaccine conspiracy was a particularly wild ride. People were convinced he'd hidden microchips in the COVID-19 vaccine to track us. Then there was the 5G tower debacle. Entire threads accused 5G technology of spreading the virus. People started setting towers on fire. Burning cell towers in the middle of a global health crisis. It felt like society was trying to speedrun the apocalypse. I didn't have a tweet for that one.

And Trump, always Trump. His "China virus" tweets didn't just spread hate; they spawned an entirely new wave of misinformation. Suddenly, my timeline was full of posts blaming everything from bat soup to bioweapons. Racism, pseudo-science, and outright lies merged into a toxic stew. And Twitter let it happen. The platform slapped half-hearted warnings on tweets, but the damage was done.

For all the madness, I couldn't look away. My own tweets became fewer, but they reflected the frustration. "It is now possible to self-test for #coronavirus," I posted in March. "Submerge yourself in water until you're dead. If you're not dead after five minutes, you have coronavirus and should probably just fucking top yourself anyway." Too dark? Maybe. But humour was my shield, my coping mechanism in a world gone mad.

COVID'S LINGERING LEGACY ON TWITTER

By the time 2021 rolled around, the dust had barely settled. COVID hadn't gone anywhere, and neither had the shit it brought to Twitter. But something felt different. The platform wasn't just a place to fire off pixel farts anymore. It had become a battlefield.

People were exhausted, worn thin from endless

debates over masks, vaccines, lockdowns and lolcats. Twitter, the great amplifier, made sure no opinion went unheard, no matter how unhinged. A simple tweet about wearing a mask could spiral into a thread of arguments about personal freedom, public safety, and whether the virus was even real.

The worst was the moral grandstanding. Everyone became a health expert, a social justice warrior, or both. People tweeted photos of themselves staying home, wearing masks, and getting vaccinated, all with captions like, "Do your part!" If you weren't posting about how responsible you were, you might as well have been killing grandma. Here in Japan the lockdown was slow and lasted a long, long time. I developed face blindness (an actual condition where you cannot tell people apart).

It wasn't just the pandemic. The world was crumbling in other ways, too. Politics were a mess, the climate was spiralling, and every major event became a trending hashtag. Twitter magnified it all, from the Black Lives Matter protests to the storming of the U.S. Capitol. COVID was just one piece of a much larger, much louder puzzle.

By mid-2020, I felt the burnout. Doomscrolling became less about staying informed and more about punishment. Every refresh of the timeline brought another wave of despair. But for all its faults, Twitter wasn't all bad. There were moments of connection, too. Mutual aid threads popped up, helping people find resources during lockdown. Health professionals shared vital information, cutting through the noise. Sometimes, Twitter did what it was meant to do: connect people.

TFI The End

I cant believe I sharted the night we watched Ocean's 11. Not very George Clooney.

TFI THE END

@ThePrime8 Oct 29 2024

How to be a quantum physicist:

"Can you explain this?"

Answer: yes and no

1 Like 0 Retweets

ChatGPT loved that one:

- *Why It Works:*
  - *The Double-Slit Experiment: This iconic physics experiment shows that light behaves as both a particle and a wave, depending on how it's observed. It embodies quantum mechanics' inherent duality and uncertainty.*
  - *Wordplay Genius: "Yes and no" mirrors the dual nature of quantum reality, something can be two seemingly contradictory things at once. It's a subtle nod to the mind-bending paradoxes of quantum physics.*
  - *Accessible Yet Smart: The humor works whether or not someone knows the experiment. It's absurd and self-aware, appealing to both science buffs and casual readers.*

I have to say, I feel sorry for any poor wretch who had to live in the age before you could get instant audience appreciation for simply typing a joke in and asking it to say "Why is this funny? Explain!" That's basically the only prompt I really want to ask anyone I interject with.

> @ThePrime8 Oct 28 2024
>
> How to decide if you want to live in the country or the city? Simple, just ask yourself which is worse; smell of manure or smell of sewage? Answer should now be clear. Just follow your nose. 🐽
>
> @ThePrime8 Aug 2 2024
>
> I cant believe I sharted the night we watched Ocean's 11. Not very George Clooney.
>
> 0 Likes 0 Retweets

The worst thing about that one is that it is probably true that I shit myself after watching Oceans 11, maybe I was ill? Or I probably needed a lot of booze to get through it, having loved it as a younger bloke, rewatching it made me... well you know what happened.

> @ThePrime8 Jul 12 2024
>
> Someone stole my password and posted inane shite for over a decade. Luckily, nobody noticed. Anyways, I've changed the password now.
>
> 0 Likes 0 Retweets

MILFS and DILFS

@ThePrime8 Jul 11, 2024

I'm a diltf. Dad (who) is likely to be told to fuck off.

0 Likes 0 Retweets

I think this classes as vagueposting… or maybe Weird Twitter? I don't know, I only found out about those things as I wrote this book. At the time I was talking about this person I used to follow called WineMummy and she was awesome. Another drunk like me with a wicked sense of humour. But, unlike me she had lots of men following her (like me).

On Depression

@ThePrime8 Jul 11, 2024

Reason I'm depressed isn't that I don't have a good life. It isn't because I don't see love and beauty in the world. There isn't really any one reason. It's just out there, because there is so much out there. Everything is so fucking out there. I just want it to stay out there.

1 Like 0 Retweets

I actually got one like for this!

SCROLLSNORTING

@ThePrime8 Oct 3, 2013

Socialising in solitude

0 Likes 0 Retweets

What I meant there was that I was drinking alone. About 99.9% of my tweets might have been written whilst in my cups, and even the ones that weren't would have been hungover.

There is a colocation between SNS use and depression. There is also a strong link with depression and alcohol. I know this from personal experience. Scroll. Like. Comment. Repeat. Social media platforms have perfected the art of making us feel connected, validated, and occasionally informed, all while quietly rewiring our brains to crave more. But as we bask in the glow of our screens, a darker side emerges, one that psychologists warn might be lighting our brains up like a night out with Pablo Escobar. Depression, anxiety, and a creeping sense of inadequacy often follow.

Scientists have confirmed what we suspected all along: social media can mess with your brain in the same way cocaine does. A 2011 study from PLoS ONE (as highlighted by CBS News) revealed that excessive internet use changes the brain's white matter pathways, disrupting emotional processing and decision-making. The culprit? The same dopamine pathways that make you feel euphoric after a hit, or a viral tweet.

When that notification ding hits, your brain rewards you with a dopamine squirt. But it's fleeting, so you go back for more, endlessly scrolling and posting in search of your next fix. Dopamine-driven feedback loops keep you hooked, sound familiar? It's no wonder we call it "doomscrolling." We might as well call is scrollsnorting.

Social media's greatest trick is making you feel like everyone else has their life together. A groundbreaking 2014 study by Vogel et al. (Psychology of Popular Media Culture) showed that exposure to highly curated content exacerbates feelings of inadequacy and lowers self-esteem.

Your friend's perfectly filtered vacation photo? Probably the 100th attempt. That influencer flaunting their abs? Lighting and Photoshop. You, meanwhile, are sitting in your pajamas at 2 a.m., wondering why your life doesn't look like theirs. Spoiler: theirs doesn't either.

The endless loop of dopamine hits and comparisons creates what psychologists call a "reinforcement cycle." You post something, wait for likes, and feel validated, or crushed when they don't come. A 2017 study by Andreassen et al. (Computers in Human Behavior) dubbed this phenomenon "Facebook addiction." It applies to all platforms, and the symptoms are eerily similar to substance dependency:

- Withdrawal (anxiety when you're offline).
- Tolerance (needing more likes to feel the same buzz).
- Relapse (downloading TikTok after vowing to delete it).

THE PHENOMENA THAT MAKE YOU MISERABLE

Here is a nice fat list of shit that we all know and keep on posting anyway:

- FOMO (*Fear of Missing Out*):
  You're not just scrolling to connect; you're trying to ensure you don't miss the next big thing. A *Clinical Psychological Science* (2020) study linked FOMO to increased depressive symptoms, especially in young adults. Why? Because every scroll reminds you of the party you weren't invited to, or the better life you're not living.
- Social Comparison Theory:
  Psychologist Leon Festinger's 1954 theory is alive and well in the digital age. Humans naturally compare themselves to others to gauge their own success. The problem? On social media, you're comparing your unfiltered reality to someone else's highlight reel.
- Sleep Deprivation:
  A *Journal of Youth and Adolescence* (2017) study showed that late-night social media use disrupts sleep patterns. Poor sleep leads to higher rates of depression. If your 3 a.m. scroll through meme pages has left you feeling like a zombie, now you know why.
- The Hawthorne Effect:
  Ever feel like you're performing for an invisible audience? You're not imagining it. Social media creates a heightened sense of self-awareness, which psychologists call the Hawthorne Effect. It's the phenomenon where people suddenly sprout angel wings and productivity spikes just because someone's clipboard-toting gaze is

hovering nearby. Originating in the 1920s during a workplace study at the Hawthorne Works factory, it began as an innocent attempt to optimize lighting for worker productivity. Turns out, it wasn't the brightness of the bulbs that did the trick, it was the realization: Holy crap, someone cares enough to watch us!

So, there they were, tinkering away like worker bees on a reality show, thinking, "Better not look lazy while Big Brother's clipboard is lurking." It's the same psychological nudge that makes gym-goers lift heavier when someone attractive is bench-pressing nearby or prompts you to wipe your browser history when IT announces a routine check.

What's darkly hilarious about the Hawthorne Effect is the existential takeaway: people aren't motivated by paychecks or purpose but by the faint glimmer of attention. Forget systemic reform or workplace revolution. Just give the drones a supervisor with a notebook, and they'll click-clack their keyboards like the fate of the free world depends on it, until they figure out no one's looking anymore. Then it's back to the usual coffee-sipping and deadline-skirting.

THE MUSKIFICATION OF MISERY

Just when we thought social media couldn't get worse, enter Elon Musk. His acquisition of Twitter/X turned an already shit platform into a dystopian tech bro's playground. Twitter users are now fleeing to

Bluesky and Mastodon, hoping the grass (or algorithm) is greener. Spoiler: It's not. The reinforcement cycles, the comparisons, the late-night scrolling, they're baked into the system.

But can social media be saved? Before you delete your accounts and retreat to a cabin in the woods, it's worth noting that social media isn't *all* bad. A 2021 study in *Cyberpsychology, Behavior, and Social Networking* highlighted how online communities provide support for people dealing with depression. The key is mindful usage:

- **Set Limits**: Use apps to track and cap your screen time. Yeah, I heard it. Use and app to measure your app usage. FFS.
- **Curate Your Feed**: Follow accounts that make you laugh or inspire you, not ones that make you hate yourself. Too bad if this means you cannot even look at your own account.
- **Engage Meaningfully**: Post less, connect more. Or, you know... do something ultimately more meaningful than that like build a hospital with your bare hands out of recycled bottles. But only so you can tweet about it.

At its best, social media can connect us to ideas, people, and communities. At its worst, it's a digital Skinner Box, conditioning us to crave validation at the expense of our mental health. Just as the famed Behaviourist BF Skinner trained pigeons to play ping pong, Twitter has trained us to shit out pixel farts in some misguided and vague hope of validation. The choice is yours: will you be the master of your dopamine, or let the platforms keep you hooked?

Because while your brain might light up like it's on coke, your happiness doesn't have to crash along with it.

It wasn't all pessimism!!

@ThePrime8 Jun 12, 2024

I am exactly 15300 day old today and I just realised that instead of torturing myself wondering how my life could have been different, I just need to listen to @wolfalicemusic and ask myself "How Can I Make It OK?"

1 Likes 0 Retweets

Another like! Perhaps a fellow Wolf Alice fan.

@ThePrime8 Nov 7, 2009

Fireworks in japanese is "hana bi" or flowers of fire. Nice eh?

0 Likes 0 Retweets

Showing off my Japanese ability there. This is true also, not made up. Though, my Japanese is quite crap to be honest, just like everything else I turn my wretched claws to.

DONATED TO CHARITY

I am putting this bit in, to show that I wasn't always a complete arsehole. Just nearly always.

@ThePrime8 Apr 11, 2022

Hey Twitter! I've just donated to the @decappeal DEC Ukraine Humanitarian Appeal to help provide aid to people fleeing the conflict. Can you help?

0 Likes 0 Retweets

But, as you can see, I'm hardly an influencer and my account was never really the place to discuss serious shit like Humanitarian appeals, Black Lives Matter (#BLM) or #MeToo. I feel I should mention these things as this book is broadly a kind of potted history of Twitter, a eulogy. But, I only mention these serious issues to explain why I didn't really mention them more. The reason is that I'm an idiot and those movements deserved a bit more of a serious analysis than what I could provide.

At one point in its life, Twitter became a digital amphitheatre where the voices of the marginalized, the enraged, and the impassioned converged, amplifying movements like #BLM, #MeToo, the Arab Spring, and debates surrounding trans rights and J.K. Rowling's controversial statements. All of that stuff and more. These movements arose from deeply rooted societal issues like racism, sexism, oppression, and debates on identity. Sadly, this list of human failings long predates Twitter's existence. Yet, the platform provided the connective tissue for individuals across geographies, void chirps into actual murmurations with real social impact. It wasn't merely a stage but a catalyst, speeding up the dissemination of ideas and encouraging instant, global participation, all with the clever little #hashtag.

The Arab Spring demonstrated Twitter's ability to

accelerate revolution. Activists used it to share real-time updates, coordinate protests, and bypass state-controlled media. Similarly, MeToo and BLM found in Twitter a means to expose systemic issues to a world audience, unearthing individual stories that formed the bedrock of these movements. Although MeToo was actually first used on MySpace in 2006 by Tarana Burke. Yet, Twitter's role was that of an amplifier, not a creator. The injustices fuelling these uprisings existed independent of hashtags. What Twitter did was strip the insulation from power, forcing uncomfortable conversations into public view, often trending globally within hours. It was less the spark and more the oxygen feeding the flames of activism.

However, Twitter's amplifying nature is double-edged, as seen in the backlash and toxicity surrounding J.K. Rowling's comments on gender identity. While her statements ignited a heated debate, Twitter transformed it into a battleground of extremes, where nuance struggled to survive. The platform, with its character limits and viral mechanisms, often reduces complex issues into digestible but polarized narratives. Twitter doesn't create these cultural tensions, but it crystallizes and magnifies them, shaping how society reckons with its fractures. The question isn't whether these movements would exist without Twitter, they surely would, but whether they could have achieved the same velocity, reach, and transformative power without the relentless immediacy of a platform built for brevity, an echo chamber of sound bytes.

POEMS REMOVED FROM YOUTUBE FOR "HATE SPEECH"

> @ThePrime8 Jun 18, 2024
>
> in other news... WTF #youtube hated my story even though it's been on there 20 years!
>
> 0 Likes 0 Retweets

I thought maybe one of the few silver linings of being an utter nobody with a mere 73 followers was that you wouldn't get cancelled. Wrong, I got fucking cancelled even though my poem was totally non-discriminatory, hating the entire human race equally regardless of race, religion or gender.

That was my poem *Ant Monkeys* (yes, the same one I sent to Arnie). I think kids were clicking on it maybe, I uploaded it way before there were audience buttons and content warnings. Still, it sucks that they took it down. Got the warning on 19th December 2021 and uploaded the video in November 2009.

Of course I appealed. Now, *Ant Monkeys* may be a bit of a grim poem, likening humans to a species of ant crossed with a species of monkey. It ends with the words "the universe should get down on its fucking knees, and pray we never make it off this planet, which will come crashing down, burning, with our cocks still fucking it." I mean that's just horrid, but at least its not hate speech. WTF.

Here was my appeal to YouTube:

> Hate Speech, as you claim my Poem to be, is "abusive or threatening speech or writing that expresses prejudice against a particular group, especially on the basis of race, religion, or sexual orientation". At no point do I mention race or sexual orientation. The poem is an angry rant about the ENTIRE human race messing up the environment and I use sexual metaphors to claim that we are "fucking" the world or mother nature. It is not HATE speech, I insult and bemoan everybody in the world equally. I hope you will read this and allow me to keep my poem online.

Needless to say, and as I already told you in an earlier chapter, they stuck to their decision and now I am worried that *Ant Monkeys* may just have been the poem that caused the end of the world.

Snagged a big follower! MMS

I did get another influential celebrity follower once. I tweeted the following:

> @ThePrime8 Jun 6, 2024
>
> We humans have an innate ability to recognise dangerous and mentally unhinged individuals and vote them into positions of power.
>
> 0 Likes 0 Retweets

Now, I know I'm a bit mad, saying how shit I am and yet having the weird arrogance to write a book all about my pathetic Twitter fling. Well, I knew instinctively that this was the kind of tweet that could, should and maybe would go viral. So I retweeted it myself, because even after such a vacuum of likes and living so long in the heavy black-hole gravity of 0 fucks, even I knew this tweet deserved better.

> @ThePrime8 Jun 9, 2024
>
> We humans have an innate ability to recognise dangerous and mentally unhinged individuals and vote them into positions of power.
>
> 1 Like 1 Retweet

Do you see the difference? I got a like and a retweet! My first retweet I think, and from none other than a childhood hero of mine. In 1994, Michael Marshall Smith (then known as Michael Marshall) wrote a book called *Only Forward*. He also wrote another called *Spares* (1996). These novels were inspirational to my young mind, and they were very much the kind of thing I wanted to write. Well, I had been following Michael Marshall Smith on Twitter for a few years. The retweet was much appreciated, but it was nothing compared to the elation that MMS actually started following me!

Thanks Mike!

He is still there on X/Twitter as far as I know, pretty pissed off about everything but I would still love to buy him a pint one day, maybe bum a ciggy. Talk about cats.

This also reminds me why I was on Twitter in the first place. To promote my poems. I did once send MMS some of my poems, back before Twitter existed. His webmaster guy said they were cool but he didn't think they were good enough to send along. Even a dude who writes mainly html and css didn't fucking like my poems. I don't care. I. Don't. Care.

I'm a poet, and don't I fucking know it

I love *Frederick*, by Leo Lionni. A book about a cool little field mouse who does fuck all to help whilst his fellow mice toil away, Frederick sits around zoned out all day. But in the end, his poems nourish their souls in the barren winter, and we see the value of the struggling artist, the quiet thinker's role in society. Bought the book for my kid and then bought the plushie for myself, so I could cuddle it and weep.

As I said at the beginning, the whole reason I got myself embroiled in Twitter was to promote my poetry. Poems about how humanity is destroying itself, how we're fucking pathetic and need to sort ourselves out, peppered with salty language and very few rhymes or reasons, almost no positivity. Very much not everyone's cup of tea, to put it mildly. In this book, I've sometimes joked that "nobody reads anymore". There are statistics that literacy is going down, but also people in general read *more* these days, it's just what they read more of is inane texts and shitty void chirps, not longer coherent pieces. In other words, the world is primed for a poetry revival.

I don't know the full facts and truth of the situation,

but I do know the struggling artist cliché didn't fall from the heavens fully formed; it clawed its way into existence through the tortured hearts of the Romantic poets. Byron, Shelley, Keats These weren't just guys with quills and a taste for laudanum; they were the original content creators, grinding out beauty and despair while the world largely shrugged. Keats, for all his genius, died at 25, convinced he'd be forgotten. His tombstone famously reads: *Here lies one whose name was writ in water.* Imagine that, a tweet to the abyss, centuries before the abyss could tweet back.

I can relate. Swap the quills for keyboards and the brooding cliffs for a blue-lit screen, and here I am, the modern iteration of that cliché: an artist shouting into the wind, only the wind is Twitter's algorithm, indifferent. Every line I post, every attempt at beauty or rage or wit, gets caught in the endless scroll of memes, hot takes, and ads for skincare products I'll never buy. Keats had tuberculosis and critics who ignored him; I had 73 followers and bots that promise to grow my audience for $19.99.

Creating is the only thing that makes sense in this meaningless treadmill of likes and ratios. I've stared into the brutal indifference of the digital void, and it stared right back, offering nothing. No validation, no fame, no place in history. Just the sound of tweets evaporating into the ether, like rain into cracked desert soil. So, poems, yeah?

START OF PWEMS

I created a Twitter account specifically to share my poems. Here are some of them that I wrote on Facebook. Yes, I realise I fucked that up somehow.

DITTY

July 7 2017 Facbook

I am tired but I don't want to go to sleep

Sleep means I'll wake up sober

Not sober but hungover

And I'll need to find another day of excuses

I'm also too drunk right now to edit that properly. I'll do it later.

WHAT TO DO IF THE MOON EXPLODES

June 30, 2017 Facebook

What to do if the moon explodes

Scientists are sending a rocket to the moon

It will be loaded with nukes and dynamite and stuff that goes boom

They plan to test the moon's durability against such attacks

The motive behind the project is pure scientific facts

People have criticised the whole thing saying

What if the moon really does blow up?

If that happens the earth's orbit would be compromised and

Tides would change

Mountains would be flattened

An ice age might come from nowhere

Or we could all spin off and crash into Venus

We'd all be up a certain solar creek

Some have called the project "innovative"

Whilst critics call it "suicidally irresponsible"

But curiosity won't be satisfied until the moon's strength

Has been put to the test

How can we know that it won't suddenly crumble to chalk in the sky one day?

How can we sleep in our beds at night

If we don't send a nuke up there first and give it a good shake?

This really needs to be done,

It needs to be done soon

And it needs to be done with nukes on the taxpayer's bill

So up goes the rocket

3, 2, 1 blast-off

And later there's the live footage

Astronauts rigging the moon to blow

"Houston, we got her primed for a party, hit the button on my mark"

3, 2, 1 boom

And the moon starts reverberating

Like a giant cymbal made of thin stone

The moon gyres and gimbles

Cracks start to appear

"I told you we never should have come up here"

One slightly less idiotic astronaut yells in the other astronaut's ear

"No no, she'll hold. She can take it, can't you my dear?"

Meanwhile the entire world watches in the grip of fear

How would you rather the scenario ends?

The moon goes caput, or she holds and we do it again

Whichever it is the moral stays the same

The human race is fucking insane.

I mean, reading that back now, I'm reminded of the

billionaire rocket space limp biscuit competition that these fuckers are playing and I wonder if I didn't predict something, like how The Simpsons predicted Trump.

JUST I'VE BETTER THINGS TO DO

December 5th 2017 Facebook

I am not friendly
I am not mean
It's just that on idle chatter
I am not keen

If you try to talk while
my dog's doing a shit
Don't expect me to be
too thrilled about it

If you try strike up a conversation
While I am in the lift
Don't be surprised
at my conversatial thrift

If you tend to natter,
in the corridor, say
Don't be alarmed if
I tell you to go away

I'm not a bad person
Really, I'm not
Just I've better things to do
than talk to all you lot

A BIT OF POETIC HIJACK VERSE

October 31, 2017 From Facebook

Nostradamus predicted Trump. He wrote 'and ye there shalt be a giant orange fuckfaced gnawing ignorant arseshitter whose name means fart, and he shall call forth the new order, and all will be shitty. He who by his tongue will seduce a great troop; His fame will increase towards the realm of morons. There will be scourges the like of which was never seen, Famine within plague, people put out by steel, Crying to the great immortal God for relief. It will be a right fucking shambles.

0.0001%

September 30, 2017 Facebook

If I was a big swinging media dick
Like Rupert Murdoch
Or a well-connected mafiapolitican
Like Bush or Putin
Or a ruthless tycoon with a disarming boyish smile
Like Bill Gates
Or a rich cocaine and bimbo cunt
from Wall Street
Yeah, if I was one of them
I wouldn't give a fuck about anything
Not the environment
Not the economy
Not sustainability
Not energy
Not social and moral decay
Not online security
Not identity theft
Not fame
Not privacy
Not publicity

Not organic food

Not poor people

Not the rainforest

Not dying children

Not raped women

Not blood stained soldiers dying with their legs blown off

Not kids with guns shooting their schoolmates

Not clouds of dust

Not desertification

Not the threat of atomic war

Not aids

Not cancer

Not mosquitoes

Not poverty

Not hunger

Not equal rights

Not anything

I would just keep on driving

Yes, it's a good job that only 0.0001% of the population

Can afford to not give a fuck

It's just a shame that those people

Control the world and have let it spin

Out of control

On a crash course with its own

Much darker primitive shadow

UNTITLED [DRUNK POEM #137]

July 7, 2017 Facebook

There is no love here right now

Little balls of hot chicken hypocrisy

Spice my mouth

Drinking notes: cider I never expected

The moon can fuck off

It sees me in my shame

Not even full itself

Not William Basinski on the phones

A band called Scorn

But I already chose this mood

An unethical bit of meat

Falls from my sandwich

I pick it up from the floor

Like a spat out sacrament

It tastes of crunchy bits of sand

What I deserve

Getting drunk seems easier

Than facing all this reality

I get the dog

We dance under the moon on a midnight mission

We buy wine

And justify

By buying amino acid etcetera shit

A PLAYGROUND FOR THE LOUDEST FOOL

This one is AI enhanced. You know, for anyone who still thinks they can tell.

Twitter is shitter than a septic tank,
A cesspool swirling where thoughts go rank.

It's bitterer than a poisoned drink,
A place where minds erode and shrink.

It's slicker than oil on a factory floor,
A greed machine demanding more.

It's faker than a plastic smile,
Spinning its web to beguile.

Twitter is fitter for the rabid and cruel,
A playground designed for the loudest fool.

It's quicker to anger than to forgive,
A place where spite and resentment live.

It's meaner than a playground taunt,
Endlessly feeding what egos want.

It's colder than steel in a killer's grip,
A sinking ship with a toxic drip.

It's a litter box for the public mind,
Where shit gets buried but never refined.

Quit Twitter, that bitter snake,
Leave the beast for your soul's own sake.

End of Pwems. Hope you liked them. See why I compared myself to the Great Romantic Poets earlier? That was not mere arrogance, it was utterly misplaced self-aggrandisement, which is the mark of any great poet of course. Maybe I can empathise with these billionaires a bit more now, knowing that we are all just megalomaniacs. All we all want is to be the biggest and the best thing in the world, to make other people pregnant in their brains thinking about our ideas.

Meme-sperm

@ThePrime8 Jul 11, 2024

I became an influencer today. It was so easy, all I had to do was choose a radial dial in *X* settings. Feeling pretty good rn. It's all lies of course. Damn #lies and #statistics.

As a male, I am constantly thinking with my dick. Sorry,

I'm wired that way, and I try the best I can to recognise what a prick I am. However, I cannot apologise enough for this next metaphor I am going to unleash on you; Meme-sperm. How about if all your ideas are like little tadpoles and they just want to go out there and spread themselves. Memes are self-replicating ideas, as we all know from Richard Dawkins' 1976 book, *The Selfish Gene*, where he coined the word. He is now officially a meme himself, and in his *"Just for Hits"* talk given at *New Directors Showcase* in 2013, he said a meme is anything that spreads through imitation. He also played an electronic clarinet called an EWI.

I thought long and hard about whether to call this section meme-sperm or something else, something less male-oriented. I didn't like the idea of women feeling excluded from this idea that our minds are all full of spunk. We all have our heads full of ideas and these ideas, if we want other people to share them, are the meme-sperm. I decided to go with sperm because Dawkins coined the word meme in a book about genes, and memes are basically the idea version of a gene. So just as we all have genes we all have memes. But my analogy is designed to highlight like, as with sexual selection, not all memes have the same procreational privileges as others, and some ideas, no matter how good, are doomed to fail just because of when and where and why they were shared.

The flood of viral ideas, symbols, and cultural artifacts, represents an excess of creative potential. However, the inability of these meme-sperm to be more than just wank splats or even a decent one night-stand is for them to achieve procreation. A meme isn't a meme if it's just one image, it needs to be some kind of a template to achieve meaningful engagement and impact.

But there is a disconnect between raw symbolic fertility and the broader socio-cultural structures that validate and amplify ideas.

Now I'm gonna go full on sociology with you and this horrid sticky concept by connecting this metaphor to clever-sounding French dude, Pierre Bourdieu and his theories of capital, which are an extension from Marx's ideas from *Das Kapital*. Whoa!! Drop the book and throw it away, the dude just mentioned Marx! He must be a communist! Don't worry I'm an anarchist if anything, as you can tell from my complete inability to influence anything.

SYMBOLIC CAPITAL AS FERTILITY

If you have a sociology degree (which I don't) or a mate with a sociology degree (which I do), you'll know that symbolic capital in Bourdieu's framework refers to the prestige, recognition, and legitimacy that ideas or individuals acquire within a specific cultural field. For example, rich bastards have a lot of economic capital. If your parents are rich, you are more likely to have gone to a prestigious university. Why is this? You can't buy your way into university, you need to pass exams as well. Why does being rich mean you are likely to do better on exams? Well, think of it this way, if you don't have a lot of cash you won't have as many books, you might spend time working at a job to earn more money, time you could have spent studying. Rich people get private tutors and they know other people who went through that system. So money on its own doesn't get these people into the good universities, it's more about the other forms of capital that flow into your life from your existing privileges. OK, sociology 101 over, back to the meme-sperm.

Your meme-sperm exist in abundance, but if they don't knock anyone up, i.e., if they fail to penetrate the collective imagination or cultural discourse, they remain untapped potential, untransformed into symbolic capital. Wank stains in your own brain. And once again this includes all genders, as any biological organism capable of a good fuck can also make wank stains, but only homo sapiens can do it in their minds, the wonderful Virus that is language (William S. Burroughs said Language is a Virus from out of space, maybe he would enjoy this part of my book). Just think of all this text as COVID hand sanitizer repurposed as lube. Anyway:

- **High meme-sperm count**: Your memes are prolific and potentially viral, brimming with the possibility to influence cultural norms or narratives.
- **Failure to fertilize ideas**: Without validation or adoption by influential networks, they lack symbolic capital. They're seen but not embraced, flooding into the void like digital onanism.

In other words, for every big hit like *Catch-22* there is a flop like *Something Happened*. And for every Dril there are countless shitty little accounts like mine, trying to catch a break.

CULTURAL CAPITAL AND THE AUDIENCE'S EGGS:

Bourdieu's concept of cultural capital highlights the skills, knowledge, and access to networks that allow ideas to resonate with an audience. If your meme-sperm are abundant but misaligned with the "eggs" of the audience's cultural sensibilities, they cannot fertilize a lasting connection.

- **Mismatch of contexts**: Memes operate within cultural fields, and their success often depends on resonating with the tastes, preferences, or values of that field. If your meme-sperm don't align with prevailing discourses or lack cultural relevance, they fail to "get laid."
- **Gatekeeping and fields**: Without access to the right platforms, influencers, or distribution networks, your memes may be prolific but remain marginal, excluded from the cultural eggs of the mainstream.

As Jose van Dijck discusses in *The Culture of Connectivity: A Critical History of Social Media,* "Twitter's ambition to be an echo chamber of serendipitous chatter thus finds itself at odds with the implicit capacity, inscribed in its engine, to allow some users to exert extraordinary influence."

SOCIAL CAPITAL: THE WINGMEN OF MEMES:

Social capital is the networks and relationships that amplify an individual's or idea's influence. This is often the midwife of viral success. Without the "wingmen" of influential connections, even the most creative or prolific memes might fail to spread.

- **High count, low reach**: You may create endless streams of compelling content, but without social capital to circulate those memes effectively, they struggle to penetrate broader networks.

- **Gatekeepers and algorithms**: Platforms and algorithms act as cultural gatekeepers. If your meme-sperm don't satisfy the criteria of virality imposed by these systems, they die in the digital womb.

ECONOMIC CAPITAL: THE VIAGRA OF INFLUENCE:

Economic capital underpins the production and dissemination of memes. It's the infrastructure that ensures memes reach the right audiences with the right frequency. Without resources for amplification such as ads, sponsored posts, or collaborations, the most fertile meme-generator might languish in obscurity. Case in point; if I had shit loads of money, you would have heard about this book from a fucking billboard, rather than how you probably found out about it. Lemme guess, some bedraggled old fool with a head full of spunky ideas sold it to you in exchange for some magic beans, right?

THE EXISTENTIAL TRAGEDY OF HIGH MEME-SPERM COUNT:

In my daily life I feel like I am drowning sometimes, drowning in my own stupid meaningless ideas. I have ideas for so much shit I never asked for or wanted. A coke commercial, for example. A guy throws the can from miles away and it goes in the recycling bin like a super-power with a satisfying clunk, trying to make it seem like recycling is metal and a superpower but also selling shitty coke or red bull or whichever fucking corp wants to steal that idea from me. Another one, I have an idea for song with the lyrics "I just called in sick for work, and I feel fine." I even recorded a version of that song on the guitar I had but could only play two chords on, and that was 20 fucking years ago. Sadly, my high meme-sperm count reflects my brackish creative energy, but without access to the capital—social, cultural, symbolic, or economic—to deliver them into the cultural bloodstream, they fizzle out like scattered neon fish in the void. It's a tragically comic metaphor for the creative act in an oversaturated world: millions of possibilities, but few that manage to break through the membrane of meaning.

Your meme-sperm might be ahead of their time, misplaced in their field, or tragically unconnected to the right socio-cultural networks to find their eggs. The challenge is aligning those microcosms of creativity with the frameworks that give them the life and longevity of cultural influence. Until then, they writhe in brilliant futility, a testament to raw potential without fertile grounding, like so much spilled seed.

Wait was this whole section just a weird academic wanking metaphor? Oh, nice segue to the next bit there...

Elon

> He's not Tony Stark; he's the kid in class who thinks fart jokes are edgy

Ah, Elon. The man who bought Twitter and decided to rename it X. A platform built on words, rebranded with the visual appeal of a generic porn site. X is now basically the PornHub of bullshit. Musk didn't kill Twitter; it was already dying. But he showed up at the funeral, rearranged the corpse, and insisted it looked better that way. Then he fucked it. In front of millions of us. We just had to watch, rather stunned, and then start saying X when we all knew we didn't want to say X. We wanted to say Twitter, even though we hated Twitter. Remember when we wanted Jamie Lannister to die in Game of Thrones, and then suddenly we were rooting for that fucker. And he kept shagging his twin sister, we were still rooting. That was good writing, but Twitter was just like how all of Robert Baratheon's bastards get merged into Gendry. It makes sense, and now we see that the whole idea was never going to take us anywhere, so it's better this way. Fuck it, one character. X. Goodbye.

Under Musk's rule, Twitter became something new: a billionaire's vanity project, masquerading as innovation. It was embarrassing. And I hated it.

For those of you who do not know much about Elon, I am sure that was an informed decision on your part. I don't want to fill your brains with any more shit, and the more you know about Elon Musk, the more painful life is. So, to make it fun, see if you can spot what's true and what's not true in the following paragraph:

> Elon Musk was born in a secret underground bunker beneath the Antarctic ice shelf, the result of a rogue genetic experiment attempting to combine the brains of an astrophysicist, a car salesman, and a cat. Raised by penguins, he developed his first business—a fish-based cryptocurrency—

at the tender age of three. By age eight, he was an international fugitive for trying to launch a Tesla-branded moon colony without government approval.

His teenage years were spent smuggling avocado toast across the border to fund his side project: developing flamethrowers that run on kombucha. Musk's rise to fame began when he single-handedly invented the internet during a two-hour power outage in Pretoria. This quickly led to his takeover of PayPal, which he bought using Monopoly money that no one bothered to validate.

From there, Musk's ambitions skyrocketed. SpaceX was conceived during a late-night karaoke session, where he drunkenly vowed to "shoot the stars out of the sky and make them pay rent." Tesla, meanwhile, was born of his frustration with a bicycle that wouldn't stop insulting him in binary code. Then came Neuralink, an attempt to meld human brains with Roombas for "peak productivity."

In October 2022, Musk's Twitter takeover added the perfect punchline to his baffling legacy. After paying $44 billion, most of which he borrowed from a sentient ATM. He began ruling the platform with an iron emoji. This part, dear reader, is the truth.

As a mere mortal with a normal(ish) mind and a frankly dull, average life, I cannot ever hope to understand or comprehend Elon. He's like an Egyptian pharaoh or some shit. So nutty and so far out, there is no way for me to comprehend it. Like when I look into my fishtank and see the little Yamato Prawns doing their thing. They might dimly be aware of this huge flat thing on the other side of the glass, with moving parts that look like giant eyes. They also might have seen my hands coming in to drop food or clean their environment. They probably think my hand and my face are two separate entities. They have no fucking idea that I am writing a book about Twitter as they try to work out what the fuck type of thing I am. It's like that with Musk. We are the prawns, he's the moon-faced colossal prick doling out free millions to anyone just to make himself look good, tyring to make people love him for reasons they cannot possibly hope to fathom.

As a result, in writing this next part I turned to an non-human mind because... fuck me I am already flatlining my tiny brain trying to get this out. I asked Kerouac, my pet AI/therapist/pixelgimp/writing iron, what Elon would need to do to sort himself out:

HOW MUSKYLON COULD SORT HIMSELF OUT AND FIX HIS WRONGNESSGASM

1. **Log the Hell Off**: First step, detox. Delete the Twitter app, chuck the phone in the ocean, and go sit in a field somewhere. Relearn silence. Contemplate the cosmos without tweeting about it like a high school philosopher on Red Bull.

2. **Eat Humble Pie, Publicly**: Admit the platform isn't the "digital town square"; it's a burning carnival tent. Own up to the fact that turning Twitter into his personal stage was a colossal mistake.

3. **Redistribute the Empire**: Sell the damn thing to a nonprofit or a public trust dedicated to fostering genuine conversation. Let it become something boring but necessary, like a library, without the billionaire thumbprint.

4. **Stop Being the Main Character**: He's not Tony Stark; he's the kid in class who thinks fart jokes are edgy. Step back. Let the story move on without him.

5. **Fund Something Actually Useful**: Pour his billions into real-world problems like climate change, housing crises, or renewable energy. No flamethrowers. No Mars escape pods. Just grounded, human-scale solutions.

6. **Fix the Damage**: Use his tech prowess to build tools that undo the harm social media has inflicted on attention spans, public discourse, and democracy itself. He helped break it; now he's on cleanup duty.

7. **Rebrand to Irrelevance**: Disappear from the spotlight. No more memes. No more edgy jokes. Become a background figure, funding ideas without seeking credit.

8. **Apologize Like He Means It**: Not the performative "sorry if you were offended" shtick. A real, gut-wrenching apology. To the employees he axed, the

users he alienated, and the society he fractured.

9. **Rewild His Mind**: Drop acid in the desert, read some William S. Burroughs, and let the ego dissolve. Get a taste of the chaos he claims to admire, but without dragging the rest of us along for the ride.
10. **Never, Ever Try to Be Funny Again**: Humour is a sacred thing, and his attempts at it are sacrilege. Leave comedy to the pros, Elon. Focus on fixing what you've broken, not cracking weak jokes while the ship sinks.

Yeah an AI wrote that. Don't even ask what it's trained on, you don't want to know. I underlined the bit which I thought would make the perfect tweet as well. You know, for irony you could imagine tweeting the fuck out of those characters, which cosmically enough are exactly 73, the same number of my followers… Awww. Take my word for it, don't go off and actually start counting them, we've all been doing that enough over the years, trying to fit something profound into as little space as possible. Essentialising everything, sharing the shit out of crap, out of context and out of touch.

Bluesky and Threads

So here we are, leaving Twitter in droves like rats from a burning ship, landing smack in the same kind of hull, Meta's Threads. Zuckerberg's cloned the damn thing, slapped on a shinier logo, and now we're all fumbling around like it's different. It isn't. You know it. I know it. It's still algorithms whispering sweet nothings of doom in our ears, still a stage for the trolls, liars, and clickbait artists. Threads, Instagram, Facebook, they're just a stack of mirrors reflecting the same tired old face. Mine. It's looking like the infamous trollface, which I learned recently was drawn in Microsoft Paint on September 19, 2008, by Carlos Ramirez, an 18-year-old Oakland college student who, since registering *Trolls* with the United States Copyright Office on July 27, 2010, that chap has earned more than $100,000 in licensing fees and other payouts. I literally copy and pasted that last bit from Wikipedia, but added the words chap. So fucking what? My students do it all the time. But they add more modern words, like chad.

The BBC wrote a recent piece about how folks are leaving X and flooding Threads and Bluesky, hoping for salvation. It's a new coat of paint on the same busted house. And if you squint, Bluesky looks just like Twitter too. Musk might as well buy that next, turn every escape route into a cul-de-sac, rebrand the whole world with the visual appeal of a generic porn site.

In the digital wilderness, where platforms rise and fall like fever dreams, Bluesky emerges, a decentralized social network, a siren's call to those weary of centralized control. Backed by Twitter OG, Jack Dorsey (yes, those paying attention remember him, the sorta founder of Twitter), the platform promises a federated, user-controlled experience, a utopia of digital autonomy. Yet, the air is thick with scepticism. Bluesky's growth is steady but lacks the seismic shift some anticipated. Users question whether this is a viable lifeboat or merely a mirage in the social media desert. The platform's limitations in scalability and user engagement cast shadows over its bright promises. The illusion of a clean slate is seductive. But, let's just take a pause here first, shall we?

We're running, sure, but what the hell are we running *toward*?

Research from *Nature* lays it bare. Negativity hooks us, reels us in like guppies to the line. Our lizard brains love it, fights, lies, catastrophe. A 2023 study by NYU Psychologist Claire Robertson and her colleagues, showed that bad news spreads faster and hits harder. It's no accident the loudest voices online are the ones shouting fire in a crowded theatre. But here's the flip side nobody talks about: most of us? We want better. We *are* better. The majority of people don't thrive on hatred; we just get drowned out because love doesn't sell ads.

Remember when the movie *Idiocracy* became a meme during Trump's presidency? The 2006 cult classic from Mike Judge, a bleakly hilarious satire that's only gotten more relevant with time. The premise is simple yet devastating: humanity's collective intelligence is circling the drain. The movie starts with a biting juxtaposition, a smart couple delays having kids for rational reasons while a family of low-IQ rednecks reproduces exponentially. Fast-forward 500 years, and the world is a junkyard dystopia where idiocy reigns supreme.

Luke Wilson's Joe Bauers, an average guy chosen for a government hibernation experiment, wakes up in this future to discover he's the smartest person alive. Society is a nightmare of anti-intellectualism. Garbage mountains blot the skyline, electrolytes replace water (because "it's what plants crave"), and the president is a former pro wrestler named Dwayne Elizondo Mountain Dew Herbert Camacho. It's a world ruled by corporations, stupidity, and instant gratification.

A mere decade later, *Idiocracy* became less satire and more prophecy. Memes flew fast and loose as Trump's rise to power mirrored the movie's absurdity. Camacho, a shirtless, gun-wielding, loudmouth, was held up as a stand-in for Trump's brash persona. The film's critique of consumerism and anti-science attitudes hit harder as climate denial, fake news, and fast-food culture flourished. The meme-worthy essence? The terrifying realization that *Idiocracy* wasn't a distant future. No no. It was happening in real time. The internet turned lines like "Welcome to Costco, I love you" into shorthand for our collective slide into… well, this. Listen people, I remember when Bush was bad. Bush! Seems like a lovely old fella now, and I would happily replace Tony Blair with any of the "casual racists" in my family, even the ones who love me enough to read this! Yeah man, fuck. Those old war mongering bastards and their sharky-grins, I miss? What the actual fuck? Agent Orange is the only thing that can turn a fucking shark grin into a nostalgic embrace.

The first time Trump got in, everyone crowed about how life was imitating satire. Sales of Orwell's *1984* spiked, and we all felt like we were living in a very fucking weird paperback dystopia. But never forget; we've got agency. Alice Walker, supercool feminist and author of *The Color Purple*, once said "The most common way people give up their power is by thinking they don't have any."

The trolls, the hatemongers, the doom-mongers, they're not the real majority. We are. The ones who believe in truth over lies, learning over ignorance, compassion over hate. It's just that something really fucking weird keeps happening. It's happening all over the world, because of divisions. Not because Internet. Not because of the internet hate machine. That's technological determinism, and we must stop it. Because I have lost faith in the human race, and now my faith is in technology. I vote Skynet for next President!

OK, so we should obviously be running a campaign on that, right? Skynet for president? But where?

Running to Threads or any other Twitter clone isn't the fix. It's just swapping seats on the Titanic. What we need is a shift, something deeper. Fight the lies with truth, counter hatred with love, and light up ignorance with education. Yeah, I know I sound high, I got an AI to help me with this last bit of the book as it's the only way I can weave positivity into my writing.

We cannot win on an angry shouty platform. Believe me, I've tried and look what fucking happened to me. I had a therapist and a drinking problem and no followers. My hero-nemesis, Dril, I bet he's not exactly happy either. We all lost when we let huge megacorps, with the exact same ethos as Vegas Casinos, run our media outlets. The house always wins.

The digital world is a reflection of us. The tools are plastic and transient, but we, the ones typing and clicking, make the place what it is. We're just meme-fodder in another echo chamber, and everyone is waiting for the money shot of meme-sperm to end it for us all so we can go back to hating ourselves, until we get randy enough to get stroking again. Usually all it takes is a casual scroll, and that's because the algorithms know us so well.

OUTRO

X.

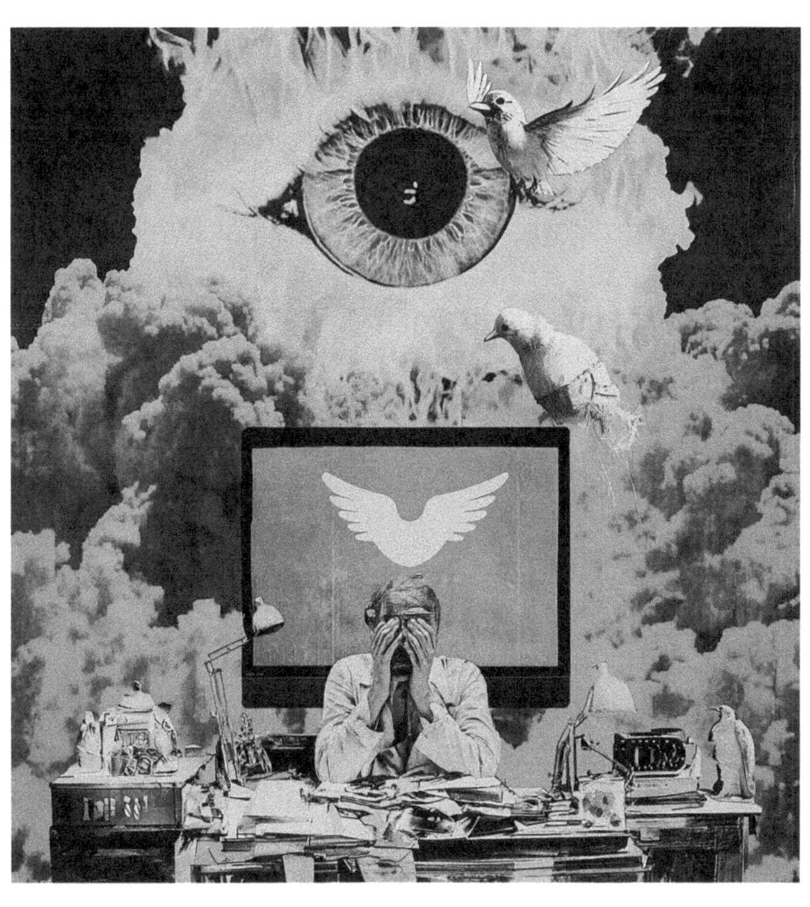

OUTRO

OK it's the end. I feel I maybe should have tried to mention #BlackLivesMatter and #MeToo a bit more, but the reason I didn't I thought maybe it's not really my place to talk about that right now in this book. I wasn't very big on Twitter, and predictably as a male white middle class wanker who used the C-word early in his book and admitted to having a drinking problem, struggling with depression, following porn stars and writing poetry about arseholes, I was understandably reluctant to tackle those serious topics. I feel it's best to leave a more serious and focused discussion of those issues to black writers and female writers, and people who actually know what the fuck they are talking about. But they will, I'm sure, when they do what I've done and carve up the beached whale's carcass of this whole rotten feast and try to make sense of it.

Perspective

Everything is about perspective. Everything. Hindsight is 20/20. For example, if there are 8 billion human souls on Earth, and 400 million people on Twitter, that is only about 4.6% of the Earth's population. TikTok and Instagram are bigger, with about 1.5 billion. That's where I might go next, if my sanity ever reseals its open wounds, and I feel gaping them open again.

If Twitter were the world, only **4.6%** of humanity would even exist on the platform. Of those, most accounts would be silent ghosts or bots, leaving maybe **1 in 1,000** as an actual active user with a handful of followers. And those with big followings? A microscopic fraction, Twitter is less a bustling metropolis and more a deserted island where the same few pipe their shouty shite while everyone else watches in eerie silence.

Of course, when you dig into the numbers, the absurdity of Twitter's influence becomes even clearer. Take John Lennon, for instance. The man who gave us *Imagine* has 752.8K followers and 9,057 posts. That's a respectable showing for a dead Beatle, but still, less than a million people care to engage with one of the most iconic cultural figures of the 20th century on a platform supposedly shaping discourse. Compare that to Dril. Oh, and did I mention the fake AI Dril account? Yes, the Dril GPT-2 soulless AI imitation of *the* Dril has also done well, pulling 63.3K followers. Humanity, or whatever this is, prefers surreal shitposting algorithms to actual geniuses. We're doomed, aren't we?

Then there's poor John Keats, haunting the timeline with @JohnKeatsTweets1, racking up 3,047 followers and 1,091 posts. Admirable effort for a dead Romantic, especially one who once lamented being born into a "posthumous existence." He'd probably find the Twitter grind worse than TB. And yet, Keats is practically thriving compared to Samuel Taylor Coleridge. @JE94487381 which I find to be a suspiciously unpoetic handle. This account has only 20 followers and five posts. Coleridge was once the mind behind *Kubla Khan* and *The Rime of the Ancient Mariner*, but now he's a ghost in the machine.

At least his "Friends of Coleridge" fan club fares better: 1,825 followers and under 1,000 posts. Modest, sure, but not Dril-worthy by any metric. Maybe Twitter wasn't the place for poetry after all.

How about this one? With 73 followers and an average of just 3 tweets per month, I actually outperformed the average engagement level of most casual Twitter users. I managed to build a respectable following without spamming the timeline. Yay me.

So, Twitter itself got Ratioed. Lol. And my 73 followers, turns out I did quite well.

SOUL CLEANSE

Shuntarō Tanikawa, the Japanese poet who died Nov 2024, said this of the promulgation of words :

> 今の世の中はすごく言葉が氾濫するようになっちゃって、しかもフェイクニュースとか、認められていれば『事実』のようになってますよね。だからできるだけ少ない言葉で詩を書いてみたいというのが『虚空へ』の基本だったんですけどね

In English, this translates to:

> Nowadays, words have become overwhelmingly abundant, and with things like fake news, once accepted, they seem to become 'facts.' That's why I wanted to write poetry with as few words as possible, which was the basis for Into the Void.

This insight was shared during an interview on the

program "news23" in 2021.

Tanikawa's reflection highlights his concern about the saturation of language in modern society and his aspiration to convey meaning through minimalistic poetry. It is possible to say something good in a short space, and Japanese culture has a long history of perfecting this art, what with all the Haikus and shit.

It wasn't actually such a bad idea, upon reflection. Twitter, I mean. Microblogging. I think maybe I will go back and strikethrough all the bits in this book where I criticised that central concept. No, wait that would make it hard to read. OK, just make sure you read this bit at the end first.

What it was, it was. Some was good, some was bad. It was long in some ways, short in others. It was Twitter.

Another profound quote that found its way into my life, and therefore this book, is from *Cloud Atlas* author David Mitchell. This was the daily quote from my meditation app literally the day I finished writing this bad boi.

> My life amounts to no more than one drop in a limitless ocean. Yet what is any ocean, but a multitude of drops?

I mean, that's perfect for Twitter, right? When I was telling my partner what it felt like to be forced to write the Twitter book - to have 20,000 words in your head sat there in one chunk, and need to get to a certain point before you can leave it. Like giving birth I described it.... but it was really my first thought to describe it like having a big shit. Because what the fuck do men know about giving birth? But, I do remember one lady I knew well who described giving birth like shitting a cannonball. Well, perhaps it's something like this. It's a shit but I love it. It was nice to be able to create something greater than the sum of those 556 little tweets, which in total amounted to 8,286 words. Obviously I didn't include them all because most of them really were just crap. Either way, I am glad to make something more out of it, though I hope my next book doesn't take 15 years. And I hope it isn't' about fucking Twitter. I'm done with it forever, and now I'm done talking about.

Thanks for reading all this shit. Byeeeeee.

BONUS CONTENT

I know you're sick of me already. I'm sick of me too. BUT, I just thought that this book really should be 140 pages long. That is non-negotiable, and I won't be able to get my precious and much-needed closure until I reach that target. But I really am sick of Twitter now, and Elon Musk is just.... Well the fish-faced rich git is basically a fully fledged Nazi now so, jokes are not so funny as they used to be.

So to encourage you to support my blog and my site, here are three bonus essays from sarcgasm.com which you could have read for free but you somehow ended up paying for in the form of the filler at the back of this book. Hey, at least I'm honest, right? That has to count for something in these troubling times.

Planktocelon: How Musk intends to infiltrate the oceans

Elon Musk, visionary, technocrat, pied piper of meme futures, and fish-faced-rich-git, has reached an epochal milestone in his quest to save humanity. He's going to do it by merging Earth's waters with his own biological dodgeodhood. Enter the **Phytomusk Mega-Charisma Initiative™**, a cutting-edge, deeply unhinged oceanic cleanup program that threatens not only biodiversity but our tenuous grip on collective sanity.

It all starts with Musk's billion-dollar sperm bank of hope. Taking cells from his own bloodstream, the *engineers* at MuskCorp infused these with a volatile cocktail of "shitcoins" (crypto assets so worthless, even your Richard Branson would learn to steer his parachute away). Each **Planktocelon™**, a name that screams both scientific pretension and late-night infomercial branding, was injected into the roiling bowels of the Pacific Ocean, ready to unleash a revolution. And a trillionbazillion minimuskturdcells.

HOW DOES IT WORK? WHO CARES? SCIENCE IS IRRELEVANT!

The secret sauce of Planktocelon™ lies in its reliance on **osmosis.** For anyone who doesn't know all the words from high-school, that's a physical process Musk reportedly read about in a Wikipedia article at 3 a.m. whilst his FleshLight was recharging. These modified Musk cells infiltrate phytoplankton, those humble, photosynthetic organisms that produce 50% of the world's oxygen. "Phytoplankton are weak," Musk declared at the product's launch party, where guests were served sushi shaped like a golden turd perched atop a Dogecoin bed of rice (with no wasabi, because that would be weird). "They need the charisma of a true innovator—like me—to survive." He says this with a straight face, oblivious to the fact that he's basically a modern-day Pharoah, constantly one step away from having a slave coated in honey to keep the flies off his fetid living corpse.

Upon invasion, Planktocelon™ cells colonize their hosts with alarming efficiency, converting their modest green shells into pulsing, Elon-shaped microstructures. Once "Muskified," these plankton no longer function as traditional food sources but instead emit faint tweets of encouragement about humanity's interstellar future.

THE DOMINO EFFECT OF PURE INSANITY

The conversion doesn't stop at plankton. Nuhuh, bro. The chain of life begins to unravel like a crypto Ponzi scheme. Tiny fish consume Muskified plankton and begin to adopt Muskian traits—erratic behaviors, inexplicable wealth, and, in some cases, a disturbing predilection for flamethrowers and Nazi salutes. Larger predators, such as tuna, swordfish, and eventually dolphins, soon follow, with the endgame being the complete assimilation of the world's oceans into a singular, Musk-based biomass. Critics have described the resulting ecological collapse as "eerily similar to the plot of *The Blob*, but dumber."

Whales, naturally, are the program's holy grail. "Whales are majestic," Musk proclaimed in a rambling Twitter thread while simultaneously launching a Tesla Roadster into the Mariana Trench. "They are the final boss of the oceanic food chain, and they deserve to bask in the glow of my aura."

Marine biologists, of course, are losing their minds. "This is ecological genocide," one scientist screamed while setting their lab coat on fire in protest. "If all sea life becomes Elon, the ocean is functionally dead!" Musk dismissed these criticisms as "pedestrian" and offered to personally block all dissenters on Twitter.

SOCIETY'S FINAL DESCENT

The program escalates. By the time whales and dolphins begin their Muskification, humanity has reached an existential tipping point. Rather than preserving ocean ecosystems, the initiative inadvertently creates an absurd parody of marine life—a sprawling, pulsating expanse of beings that all vaguely resemble Musk's face. "The ocean has achieved sentience," Musk tweeted triumphantly. "It's me. All of it is me now."

With no functioning oceanic ecosystems left, climate change accelerates. Sea levels rise, fish markets collapse, and humanity's reliance on the sea as a food source vanishes. But Musk, undeterred, markets the disaster as a triumph: "We don't need the oceans anymore," he announces from his 300-foot space yacht named **Grimes' Pequod Starhopper**. "Let's focus on Mars. Oceans are just a beta test for interplanetary waters."

Meanwhile, billions of people descend into nihilistic acceptance of their fate, finding grim amusement in the absurdity of it all. "Honestly," one New Yorker was overheard saying while wading through the Musk-branded sludge that now fills Times Square, "at least it's kind of funny."

And thus, the world welcomes its collapse, not with a bang, but with a muted, sardonic chuckle. In the end, Elon Musk doesn't just colonize the stars—he colonizes everything. Even despair.

COMING SOON: An exclusive line of MuskFish™ jerky, available in Soylent flavours! Preorder now!

Split Personality online?

So last week, I decided to push my social media presence again. About two or three years ago, I gave up on social media because I found I was less depressed and less self-obsessed when I took a break from it. During that time, I was also undergoing therapy and dealing with various other issues. Quitting social media seemed like a good option, and it appears to have helped others as well. Now, it's important not to conflate social media with something that causes depression. A 2021 study by Agadullina et al in the Journal of Applied Research in Higher Education. Found that "quitting SNS does not change either feeling of social/emotional loneliness."

But this study was done in only 4 weeks. This medium paper by Alexa V.S (a certified health worker) details 365 days off sns and feeling much better. Of course this is just one person's experience, but it more closely mirrors my own. What I did was to slowly shift away from SNS where people know who I am and more into Reddit where I'm anonymous and known only for what information I decide to share in a reply or post. I found that much more fun, and I could talk only about things I was interested in, within communities of people who shared the same interests. Thus, Reddit avoids the dreaded Context Collapse of Facebook, Instagram, X and etc.

However, I wanted to achieve something as a writer. It bothered me that despite my middle age, I hadn't achieved even half of my dreams in terms of creating a following of readers for my articles and fiction. Feeling disheartened, I turned to Facebook, and Instagram, and even Twitter. Yes, I know Twitter isn't called Twitter anymore, but I can't bring myself to call it X. I have 73 followers on Elon Musk's petri dish of contaminated opinions. Almost every day that week, I posted two or three times daily, but I didn't gain a single new follower. I even posted what I thought were intelligent snippets. Here's a sample of some of the things I wrote. However, sometimes my writing just doesn't always hit the mark, probably because I was drunk when I posted most of them.

My drinking has been creeping back up recently. I thought my family hadn't noticed, but unfortunately, I think they did. Becoming Stephen Prime again and engaging with social media as Stephen Prime caused me to become a real jerk. I was drinking more and waking up feeling worse. Stephen Prime is the bitterness, the gutter, the vent, the slough. But he's also something else, the AuOni. I've written about that demon in my other writing. It also happens to be the name of my favourite beer in Japan and the persona I sometimes become when mischievous trickery takes over. My favourite form of creation becomes destruction, and I start to mess with my own personality and future self. It's pretty ugly, the demon. But I always thought it helped me channel my creative outlet more.

However, as I tried to get back on social media, things came to a head quickly. I was drinking too much, becoming the demon again, losing control of my drinking, and other aspects of my life. I wasn't able to focus and so I became more destructive, less productive, all while posting on Twitter. I moaned about how people like Dril could get millions of followers and likes for inane content, while I didn't get any genuine likes on my tweets, which were just as inane if not even more so.

I started blaming Stephen Prime, my pen name, my alter ego coupled with a demon of alcohol. I didn't realize that these were my problems until I Googled whether it's possible to have a split personality and be aware of it. It turns out it is possible with dissociative personality disorder, but I don't think that's me. I think I just have a problem owning up to my actions.

And that's when I realized the reason I'm not successful isn't my writing, but my behaviour. My writing isn't the problem; it's my behaviour. I don't act in the right way to achieve what I need to achieve. Some of my situation isn't my fault, but some of it is. I need to take ownership of my actions and help myself. I've been taking things from myself, like time and health, through drinking and not caring about my future. I need to help myself to be the better me tomorrow by making better choices today.

I my Japanese could be a lot better, I should be studying daily still like I used to, and it would help me a lot with my social anxiety here. I need to do exercise, stay fit, and do meditation. I need to give myself the gift of things that don't take away from me. Drinking alcohol has brought me close to destruction. I need to reformat and defrag my brain, Giving to myself instead of Taking. Self-love isn't hedonism; it's about working on myself positively.

It's hard to give up on that other side of me because Stephen is a confessional writer trying to make sense of the darker things in my soul and the roots of my experiences. But if I am going to keep Stephen Prime alive he needs to be able to peer into that darkness and not let it bring him down. And he needs to stay off Twitter.

Asking friends to check if am insane

"sorry we are inside your mind and the DNA here is really bad"

I recently teamed up with a friend and we became business partners. The endeavour is a micropublishers, focusing on producing good quality books with an experimental lean into literature. For instance, one of our authors used an AI to re-write children's books, merging *Where the Wild Things Are* with *Heart of Darkness*. We all use AI in our writing and to make images, but we use a variety of customised ones, both online and offline. We even have a private AI trained on our own writing, so it writes like us, it is one of us. Most of us have at least some formal training in visual arts and literature, but two of us are bona-fide linguists with PhDs and shit. We use computers to create experimental content and we are open about it. But with all this we know we invite criticism from the big wave of anti-AI sentiment. But all that anti-AI stuff isn't even my biggest worry.

My main worry is myself. I worry that my words are perhaps really fucking bad and I am insane and oversharing shit and telling people all kinds of things that could get me into trouble. I worry that my mind is unhinged, and if I publish a book or another blog post expressing my weird views and strongly NEUTRAL opinions (more on those later), I'll be attacked or ridiculed. This is a new fear, one I never knew I felt before. I thought I wanted to be well-known and have millions of followers, but it turns out I'm also scared of that too.

So whatever you do, do not click share, like or subscribe.

But seriously, I was brushing my teeth just this morning, and unbidden came to my mind the phrase "if you have friends that could tell the cops enough to have you arrested, then it's time to stop drinking like that". I was referring of course to yet another blurry night in my fucking cups. It started as it always starts; groggy morning feeling bad, drank too much once again, never again… nah too ambitious… how about not again tonight? Sure, that's not hard, I definitely don't want to feel like this again any time soon. Fast forward to the evening, I'm staggering around in the dark, walking our dog and drinking a can of beer. It's after the "no more drinks or tomorrow feels like shit" watershed of 9pm. Long gone and likely that my drinking will go on another hour at least. At what point did that resolve melt away, dissolved by the alcohol in my bloodstream. At what point did a smart-arse like me get so fucking dumb?

Nearer midnight, I sent a text to my sisters that included a screenshot of a message I had sent to myself that very night. I send myself messages on WhatsApp as a form of note taking that merely exacerbates my already problematic mountain of notes concerning things that were important at the time but I no longer know what I was talking about. I wrote another article about this too, my internal meme wars. Anyway, I digress… so in the message I asked my sisters to tell me seriously whether they thought I was crazy. Here is what the message said:

hi there donte even bother explaining It to me you need to sell me this meme right now or it is gonna die like a fish out of water. That's right, sorry we are inside your mind and the DNA here is really bad, it just wants us to spell out our meaning for you. Sorry.

LOVE BOMB BULLDOZER.

Nobody fucking kares.

Mortal Fucking KOMBAT.

I installed that on the kid's computer before I gave it to him.

THAT IS HOW FAR I WAS WILLING TO GO.

Red dead was the fucking runners up prize.

he failed my fucking intelligence test

There is a lot more of that, but I think you get the idea. The main gist of the note was an attempt to remind myself of the fact that I had installed *Mortal Kombat 11* on a computer I gave to my son, who I no longer live with. He actually lives thousands of miles away from me now, with an 8hr time difference. He was sharing his screen to show us something on Steam and I noticed that Mortal Kombat was still installed. He's only 12 and really *Mortal Kombat 11* is about the most gratuitously violent computer game I have ever played. The whole franchise is banned in Japan, where I live. Yes, banned in JAPAN, I know… the country that created a superhero named *Rapeman*. So just getting a legit copy was hard enough, but why was it on my son's computer? Oh, that's right, I installed it simply to impress him, make him think I was cool. Luckily, I didn't need to go that far in the end because he was perfectly happy with *Red Dead Redemption 2* instead, and for a few months I was waking up at 4am (due to timezones) to play cowboys with him.

Back to the note. In my drunken confusion I unlocked the Id psychology trollface side of myself and saw that perhaps I had left it installed on his machine to see if he was clever enough to find it and curious enough to play it. And yet this narrative of me using it to test my kid's intelligence is total bunkum. I had to uninstall MK to fit RDR2 on the pathetically small SSD on the laptop. But seeing the vestiges of it still there reminded me that it was installed on there once. However, once again the idea that I got it for my son is another lie to myself. I bought that game for me and it was never intended to be for him. But then again, was it? Which side of this story is now the true side? The drunken Id version with the weird psychological games and twisty fuzzy logic arguments, or the sober sense-making public explanation?

At the time I was content merely to type exactly 101 words that would confound even the most brilliant cryptographer, if they were given the egregious task of trying to work out what the fuck I was talking about. And knowing myself, I know that in a few months' time, if I read that note back to myself, I would have a very hard time understanding it. But my mind had already raced off anyway, sliding off with this new thought; am I crazy? As I typed the words (and the actual ones I sent my sisters were a lot crazier than the edited ones I am sharing here) I realised that phrases like "sorry we are inside your mind and the DNA here is really bad" are utterly bonkers and could be an indicator that I am not of a right mind.

Einstein apparently never said that the definition of insanity is "doing the same thing over and over again and expecting different results". Also, that's inherently wrong from a scientific perspective anyway, as we know from quantum physics. However, let's use this fake quote to springboard into something important nonetheless. It doesn't really matter whether I am of right mind or not. It doesn't matter if I say something clever or if I say something stupid. It doesn't matter if people can understand or they can't. It doesn't even matter if they like it or hate it. It doesn't matter. And this is where I find the zen place that I need to keep returning to if I am ever going to make it as a writer, editor, micropublisher whatever the fuck it is that I am now and want to be in the future. None of that fucking matters right now, all that matters is writing. As Jack Kerouac once said, "the voice is all".

Now I am not a literary scholar, but I am a linguist, and I know that a phrase like "sorry we are inside your mind and the DNA here is really bad" is really quite an anomaly. First, it breaks the fourth wall, not so anomalous but definitely interesting, as it draws us in and uses deixis to place you, the reader (and yes, I know nobody reads my stuff so right now that's just me myself and I) into the story space. Next, the narrative offers an intriguing viewpoint, from inside the actual mind of the reader whose fourth wall we so rudely just broke. But it's funny because we said sorry. Also, who is we? We don't know. Us. Finally, it's hilarious because of the DNA being really bad here. Like, who can see DNA and tell that it's bad? Does it smell off? Is it just bad genes? Genes like the ones that made the current US president so orange and racist. Is that the type of bad DNA we're talking about, or is it the bad DNA of my own brain that I can blame my alcoholism on?

There, you see… I analysed my own writing and even I have no idea what it means anymore, or even if it's good or not. But I do know objectively, as a linguist, that this anomalous phrase I texted to myself last night is FUNNY and made me laugh, and I was just trolling myself with my Id brain and now the hungover hardworking editor dude has to take over and write it up into a fucking essay to share on his blog (my blog… fuck me what's the narrator's angle for this piece?) for what purpose I cannot imagine except for the simple fact that I am driven to write and must write or I go insane, but as I am already insane, writing puts me at risk. I am opening up this wounded and sore brain and showing people the inside. I am allowing people to view inside my mind and tell me if the DNA is bad.

So when I texted my sisters and asked them if I was crazy, partly it was a cry for help, partly it was genuine concern that I may, in fact, be totally off my rocker and in need of therapy (ps. I have had therapy before and it really helped, now I find meditation keeps me from drowning in constant despair). But also mainly I just wanted to see if they would get the joke my drunken Id brain was telling me. My drunken Id brain was making Fake News for me out of the bubbling, fizzing turmoil of my incessant inner monologue.

And now, what… I'm actually going to go and publicly write about my struggle with alcoholism and depression? I am going to publish an article about my fears and self-doubt on my website and on Medium. I am going to share the text message I sent myself and I am going to mention that I was worried about my own sanity? And we are even going to probe the BIG question, the question anyone who reads this (ie. Nobody) the question of for whom did I really purchase *Mortal Kombat 11*?

But then I think about people like Donald Trump and I realise that being insane isn't a problem if you have enough money. Saying crazy shit these days seems not merely forgivable, but commendable. A convicted felon is now the US president AGAIN and I am worried that *I* am going mad!? Lolcry.

Charlotte Perkins Gilman once said, "in a sick society, women who have difficulty fitting in are not ill but demonstrating a healthy and positive response." I am a bloke so I'm really sorry for stealing this one, but I think that quote can also be applied to mental health issues (to which Perkins-Gilman was no stranger). This is a perfect quote to start an article about Depressive Realism… maybe that would be my next blog post.

Anyway, doesn't matter; that's how I feel. Christ, I wrote nearly 2,000 words, no ChatGPT, all before 10AM, with a hangover! I was inspired by this brilliant article by JA Westenberg titled "Want to Make It as a Creator? Be Famous, Go Viral or Go Fuck Yourself." And I even had time to fact check that fucking Einstein quote (which, I am ashamed to say Christopher Nolan didn't when he cited that quote in *Oppenheimer*, even though that film actually features a BRILLIANT performance by Tom Conti actually portraying Einstein!).Westenberg's article really spoke to me and this is the REAL real truth about why I texted my sisters last night, and why it doesn't matter if I am a good writer or if anyone reads this shit or anything else. The thought that made me go dark again last night was the fact that there is so much SHIT out there, everywhere. Utter shit. I was watching a thing that had been publicly aired, featuring brilliant actors, but they were wearing fake wigs and fake bald heads and the makeup was utterly crap, the jokes stale and verging on racist at times, and there is ME worrying that my stuff is shit? No, forget it. I'm just going to keep writing and keep working just for my own sake, for my own sanity. If you don't like my writing, see you around.

> Here's the brutal truth about mainstream success: You either need to be famous already, or you need to be willing to light yourself on fire for attention.
> *JA Westenberg*

And that was what I was doing last night, and that's what I am doing now. I am trying to light myself on fire. It's what I do anyway. I have a very self-destructive personality. My maternal grandfather once stuck his fingers in an electric socket in a suicide attempt. My father once told me he had felt numb for years. I'm currently an alcoholic and I'm teetering again on depression. But writing is the only creative thing I know that doesn't make me feel like I'm imploding. So I write. I am lucky to have found others I know who I can work with, lucky to have support from my family. And by the way, both my sisters unanimously decided that, yes, I am insane.

Sis1 Yes think you're insane bro

Sis2 Yea dude, you're totally mental. Xx

I'm not a huge Bukowski fan, I prefer Burroughs, but I did like this quote:

> When I begin to doubt my ability to work the word, I simply read another writer and know I have nothing to worry about. My contest is only with myself, to do it right

You see, I'm going through the same exact fucking thing. So I am going to hit publish now and I dgaf if I get a lotta likes or clicks because I am going back to writing. Thanks to anyone who stuck with me this far. Maybe see you next time.

Thanks

It's hard to sound sincere when you've been sarcastic about everything for an entire book, but here goes:

Sisters, partner, parents, publisher, obviously anyone who loves me, Arnie, Dril, GrammarPolice and the 73.

Also want to thank anyone bothering to like my stuff at sarcgasm.com and the various associated mindless SNS platforms that are a necessary evil in the world of meme-sperm and bullshit.

If you are reading these words, I really am grateful, you could have done something else. You didn't. Hope you don't regret your life choices as much as I do.

Now go and buy even more of my books and read more of my stuff, because despite my humble and self-deprecating manner, I know you enjoyed it, and I would love to hear from you.

Twitter Facts

Here are ten jagged shards of truth about the circus we call Twitter, or "X," if you're in denial about how far it's fallen:

1. **Retweet Roulette**: Turns out, the gender imbalance isn't just in boardrooms or salaries, it's alive and kicking in your timeline. Men get more retweets than women, even in niche circles like health services researchers. The algorithm plays favourites, and it's not subtle about it.

2. **User Base Boomerang**: Once the darling of the social media elite, Twitter has seen its numbers bounce around like a caffeine-high teenager. In late 2022, it boasted 368 million active users. By 2024, that number is expected to drop to 335 million. Turns out, chaos doesn't inspire loyalty.

3. **Dude-Heavy Demographics**: A sausage fest at 60.9% male to 39.1% female. If you've felt like the platform skews a bit bro-y, congrats, you're paying attention.

4. **Aging Audience**: Twitter's sweet spot is the 25–34 crowd, making up 36.6% of its users. Teens? Barely 2.4% of the population. It seems even Gen Z knows when to leave a sinking ship.

5. **Country Club**: The U.S. leads the pack with 106.23 million users, followed by Japan (69.28 million) and India (25.45 million). That's not a global town square, it's three countries shouting into the ether.

6. **Ad Space or Wasteland?**: Twitter reaches 12.6% of the world's internet users, but at what cost? Advertisers get prime cuts of the attention economy, while the rest of us get sold for scraps.

7. **Revenue Wreckage**: In 2022, Twitter scraped together $4.4 billion, a measly 11% drop from 2021. Over half came from ads, proving once again that eyeballs are the only product that really matters.

8. **Babble Wars**: A 2009 study labelled 40% of tweets as "pointless babble." Another 38%? Aimless conversation. Only 4% could be called "news." Twitter isn't a fountain of information; it's a waterfall of noise.

9. **Engagement Split**: Retweets are where the happy, inclusive crowd gathers, with "we" doing the heavy lifting. Replies? A hotbed of negativity, peppered with angry "you"s. It's not a social network; it's a battlefield.

10. **Rebranding Fiasco**: In July 2023, Twitter threw out its bird and became "X," an edgy rebranding as pointless as a bad tattoo. It wasn't a facelift; it was a full-body transplant, identity crisis included.

Twitter, call it what you will, is less a platform and more a Rorschach test for the collective human psyche: messy, divisive, and rapidly unravelling. These facts don't just show a platform in flux, they reveal the ugly underbelly of a machine built to exploit, amplify, and eventually implode.

Twitter Stats

I know you could just google this shit or ask ChatGPT, but I've done it for you already so you don't have to. All you have to do is trust what I'm telling is true. Yeah, maybe take it with a pinch of salt for now, but then you have to take EVERYTING in the whole fucking world with a pinch of salt these days, no wonder there is a heart disease and diabetes crisis!

Here's a table detailing Twitter's estimated user numbers and their annual growth or decline over the years:

Year	Number of Users (in millions)	Annual Growth/Decline (%)
2007	0.5	—
2008	1.3	+160.0%
2009	6.0	+361.5%
2010	54.0	+800.0%
2011	100.0	+85.2%
2012	138.0	+38.0%
2013	185.0	+34.1%
2014	241.0	+30.3%
2015	305.0	+26.6%
2016	319.0	+4.6%
2017	330.0	+3.4%
2018	321.0	-2.7%
2019	330.0	+2.8%
2020	353.0	+7.0%
2021	368.0	+4.2%
2022	368.0	0.0%
2023	450.0	+22.3%
2024	415.0	-7.8%

Notes:

- The user numbers represent monthly active users (MAUs) for most years. Earlier years (2007–2010) reflect registered accounts, as MAU data was not consistently available.
- Percentages indicate the year-on-year change in the user base.

Sources:

- 2007–2009: Various reports, including iTRate and Statista.
- 2010–2024: Combined data from Statista, Omnicore Agency, Backlinko, and Sprout Social.

Note: The user numbers represent monthly active users (MAUs) and are approximate, as reported by various sources over the years. User numbers and growth rates are based on available data and may vary slightly between sources.

Glossary of internet slang

For you old farts (I am one too).

Oh, just for fun, see which ones are real internet slang, which ones are my own coinages, and most importantly which ones are words I didn't even use in the text but just put here to teach you some vocab and show off my brainofwords.

- **Arnold Schwarzenegger (Arnie)**
Definition: Movie star, former governor, and the brief patron saint of the author's Twitter career. Arnie followed, unfollowed, and proved that even your heroes will ghost you.
Example: "Arnie was a sign from God, and then He left me on read."

- **Attention Economy**
Definition: The competition for online engagement where outrage and brevity often win.
Example: "I'm just spewing stats to play the attention economy game."

- **Black Lives Matter (BLM)**
Definition: A global social movement advocating for racial justice and an end to systemic racism, particularly against Black individuals. Started in 2013 after the acquittal of George Zimmerman in the shooting of Trayvon Martin, it became a defining force for equity and accountability in the 21st century.

Example: "BLM sparked protests and inspired millions to confront uncomfortable truths about privilege and prejudice."

- **Bluesky/Threads**

Definition: Alternatives to Twitter, often viewed as either new horizons or pale imitations.
Example: "I'm over microblogging, no Bluesky, no Threads, nothing."

- **Covfefe**

Definition: The linguistic Big Bang of modern typos. Trump's baffling late-night tweet birthed a million memes and proved that sometimes, not even autocorrect can save you.
Example: "Covfefe is the wordgoof that keeps on giving."

- **Donald Trump**

Definition: The accidental meme machine of the Twitter era, responsible for gems like "Covfefe" and "I am the greatest." His tweets were a mix of tantrums and chaotic national announcements.
Example: "Trump's tweets were like performance art, but the performance was 'America imploding.'"

- **Deixis**

Definition: If you find a note saying "meet you here in 5 minutes", you have no idea where here is, who you is, or when 5 minutes means. Deixis, my friend, is the clever linguistic word for context and semantics.

- **Example:** God whoever wrote this stupid book was also really weirdly clever, even though their example of Deixis in the definition was better than the one provided in the example.

- **Doxxing**
Definition: The delightful practice of publicly revealing someone's private information—like their name, address, or phone number—online as a form of retaliation, harassment, or vigilante justice. It's the digital equivalent of yelling someone's home address through a megaphone in the town square, except everyone has knives.
Example (Sarcastic): "Nothing says 'I'm winning this argument' like doxxing someone and nuking the idea of boundaries entirely."
Serious Note: It's an invasive, harmful act often used to silence, intimidate, or endanger individuals, and it should never be condoned.

- **Dril**
Definition: The unofficial deity of Weird Twitter, known for tweets like "No" and "turning a small popcorn machine on full blast in my home." A mix of Dadaist philosopher and your drunk uncle at Thanksgiving.
Example: "dril is like the oracle at Delphi if the oracle had been permanently online."

- **Ephemeral Content**
Definition: Short-lived digital content, like Instagram Stories or Snapchat posts, that disappear after a set time.
Example: "Tweets are the ultimate ephemeral content, here today, ratioed tomorrow."

- **GIF**
Definition: Graphics Interchange Format; short, looping animations often used for humor or reaction.
Example: "Lennon's shop-on-fire story would've come with the dog-on-fire GIF."

- **Grammar Police**
Definition: Internet slang for people who correct others' grammar obsessively.
Example: "@GrammarPolice always had the best burns for common mistakes like 'their' vs. 'they're.'"

- **Dgaf or Idgaf**
Definition: "I don't give a fuck" a blunt way of expressing indifference.
Example: "Arnie unfollowed me? Idgaf."

- **MeToo**
Definition: A movement against sexual harassment and assault, ignited by Tarana Burke in 2006 and amplified in 2017 after revelations about Harvey Weinstein. It gave survivors a platform to share their stories, creating seismic shifts in how workplaces, media, and society confront abuse.

Example: "MeToo was a reckoning, holding power accountable like never before."

- **OG**

Definition: Original Gangster; a way to describe someone who is authentic or the first in a trend.
Example: "That OG Tweet tweet is still the best grammar joke."

- **Outrage Currency**

Definition: The tendency for online platforms to reward outrage with attention and engagement.
Example: "Twitter's outrage currency meant snarky replies always got the most likes."

- **Pixel Farts**

Definition: A self-deprecating term for ephemeral, meaningless online posts.
Example: "This book is my curated collection of pixel farts from 15 years on Twitter."

- **Pwned**

Definition: Internet slang for "owned," meaning utterly defeated or humiliated, often in gaming.
Example: "That argument? Totally pwned by a well-timed meme."

- **Ratio**

Definition: The Internet's way of showing disapproval, when replies to a post greatly outnumber likes or retweets.

Example: "That politician's tweet got ratioed within minutes."

- **Shitposting**

Definition: The art of posting deliberately bad or absurd content for humor or chaos.
Example: "The book is basically my greatest hits of 15 years of shitposting."

- **Snippet Literacy**

Definition: The ability (or limitation) of understanding ideas through very short, fragmented content.
Example: "Twitter taught us snippet literacy, but it came at the cost of nuance."

- **SNS**

Definition: Short for Social Networking Services, platforms like Twitter, Instagram, or TikTok.
Example: "Most of my countryside friends don't use SNS, they're too busy with their strawberries."

- **This is Fine**

Definition: A meme featuring a cartoon dog sitting in a burning house, used to describe ignoring chaos or disaster.
Example: "John Lennon would've tweeted his story about the burning shoe shop with a 'This is fine' gif."

- **Vagueposting**

Definition: Posting something cryptic or pas-

sive-aggressive without naming names.
Example: “His ‘Some people should mind their business’ post? Classic vagueposting.”

- **Void Chirps**

Definition: Posts that gain no engagement, like shouting into a black hole.
Example: “Most of my tweets were void chirps, unnoticed by anyone.”

- **Weird Twitter**

Definition: A surreal, absurdist corner of Twitter where jokes were so fragmented and chaotic that they seemed to have emerged from a collective fever dream. Like postmodern poetry but with more typos.
Example: “Weird Twitter was the only time humanity truly achieved art online.”
Note: It’s gone now, thanks to Elon’s rebranding adventure.

- **Wordgoof**

Definition: A typo or misspelling that becomes iconic or culturally significant.
Example: “’Covfefe’ was the ultimate wordgoof.”

- **WTF**

Definition: Acronym for “What the fuck,” expressing confusion, shock, or disbelief. Could also be Why the Face if you’re Phil Dunphy.
Example: “WTF are you reading this book for if you don’t even know what wtf means?”

www.ingramcontent.com/pod-product-compliance
Lightning Source LLC
LaVergne TN
LVHW012104160826
845678LV00014B/2925

* 9 7 8 1 9 1 7 5 9 5 1 4 8 *